Oracle

The Seeker Series: Book Four

By Amy Reece

Oracle

Limitless Publishing, LLC
Kailua, HI 96734
www.limitlesspublishing.com

Formatting: Limitless Publishing

ISBN-13: 978-1-68058-221-5
ISBN-10: 1-68058-221-6

Dedication

For the girls who are waiting
for their happily-ever-after.
And for the boys who are
right there with them.

Part One: Determination

Chapter One

"O waste no fears on me; look to thyself."
—Sophocles, *Antigone*

Dear Jack,

I want to come home. I know we haven't found Luc or any of his people yet, but I want to come home anyway. Is that too selfish? Would I be putting everyone in danger? Rémy is away on yet another business trip; maybe this time he'll discover something.

I finished my last exam today and turned in my last paper. I don't want to spend another year here at this university. I haven't registered for classes for next semester. I talked to my advisor at UNM and she can get me signed up for student teaching if I come home.

1

I'm still afraid, but I miss home so much. I miss you. I love you, Jack. I hope you still love me. Help me figure out what to do.
Love,
Ally

I hit "send" before I had a chance to re-read and talk myself out of it. I sighed and closed my laptop as the waiter brought me another cup of herbal tea. I preferred coffee, but I still had to limit my caffeine intake due to stress-induced stomach issues.

"Merci, Marc. Comme vous vous occupez de moi! Comment va votre femme?" My French had improved immensely over the course of the past year. I stopped by this small cafe nearly every day on my way home from the university, so I knew the wait staff fairly well, including Marc, who was a new father.

"Ah, elle est épuisée. Le bébé prend toute son énergie. Il nous empêche de dormir." Marc smiled as he said this, obviously exhausted by his new son, yet bursting with pride. I admired the newest pictures on his phone and then settled back to drink my tea as he hurried away to wait on other customers.

As I sipped, I thought over the events of the past year: Rémy, Mina, and I had rushed here to Rouen soon after Michael's funeral to alert the Conseil des Voyants to the danger that Luc, one of their members, posed as he attempted to force the Seers to use their abilities to gain political power. Rémy had spent the last year traveling for his family's import/export business and looking for any hint of Luc's whereabouts. He had found several tantalizing clues, including the name Les Dépaysés, supposedly what Luc and his cronies were calling themselves, but nothing about where they might be hiding. The name roughly translated into 'displaced from one's home or country,' which made me angry, because they had displaced themselves, if anything! Nobody asked them to try to take over the Seers and grasp for power. We were incredibly frustrated with the lack of progress, but Kate and the rest of the Conseil didn't seem as disturbed as I thought they should be. I knew she was happy to have her grandson home and to have unlimited access to the heir apparent to the Oracle, whichever one of us that might be.

I tried to relax as I watched people hurry by on the busy street. A young mother pushing a stroller stopped and sat at the table next to me, motioning to the waiter for a coffee. She wilted in her chair only to sit up again and fuss with the sleeping baby's blanket. She noticed me watching and we exchanged smiles in that universal way of women admiring a beautiful baby. I looked away and sighed. Would that ever be me? I was twenty years old, living in a foreign country, and I was lonely. Jack and I communicated every day—text, FaceTime, email, etcetera—but it wasn't enough any more. I needed to be with him: to hold him, kiss him, live with him, and yes, sleep with him. I was ready to move on with my life, but this unresolved situation with Luc was holding me back. As if I had conjured a response with my thoughts, my phone dinged a text notification. It was from Jack and consisted of a two word response to my email:

Come home.

I smiled and reached to wipe away a tear as I prepared to text him back.

"Cherié! I thought I might find you here!"

"Rémy! You're back early!" He kissed both my cheeks before taking the chair opposite me. I noticed he and the young woman at the next table giving each other a once-over and rolled my eyes at him.

"What?" He shrugged.

"You just can't help it, can you?" I laughed. "Flirting is like breathing with you, isn't it?"

He shrugged again and caught Marc's attention to order a beer. "Where's Mina? I tried to get her on her mobile, but it went straight to voice mail."

I cocked an eyebrow at him and smirked. "She turns it off when she needs to concentrate. I'm sure she's at home working. Drink your beer and then we can go see her." Although we had all improved our mental communication abilities over the past year, we had also agreed to respect each other's privacy to a much greater degree, only invading each other's thoughts in the case of a true emergency, which had not happened so far this year. In fact, this year had been mostly an exercise in boredom, filled with school, training, and waiting.

***

"So what have you decided?" Rémy asked as we walked toward the apartment I shared with Mina. Both were well aware of my desire to return to the United States and were trying to be supportive of whatever decision I might make.

"Did you find anything?" I asked instead of answering his question. I hoped his early return was because he couldn't wait to tell us what he discovered. My hopes were dashed as he shook his head sadly.

"Sorry, cherié. It was a complete dead end and I came back as soon as my meetings were finished. So?"

"I need to go home, Rémy. Jack wants me to." I kicked a pebble into the street as I stopped to gather my thoughts. "I'm still afraid, but I can't hide here any longer. I have a life waiting for me back home. At least, I hope I still do."

"Of course you do, Ally. Jack is like a faithful dog waiting for you to return. Oww!" He rubbed his arm where I punched it.

"You don't have a whole lot of room to talk, buddy. *'Where's Mina? I've been home for five whole minutes and I can't reach her!'*"

He ducked his head and smiled a bit shamefacedly. "Yes, well…never mind. And if I really sound like that I'm going to go shoot myself."

"Yes, that's exactly what you sound like. I have a gift for mimicry." I tried to maintain a superior tone and a straight face.

He laughed out loud. "No, you definitely do not. And I'm simply concerned about Mina's safety, the same as I am about yours. It's my job to protect both of you. That's all."

I stopped again and stared at him. "I worry that you're actually starting to believe that, Rémy. Plus, we don't know for sure you are the Shield the prophecy mentions. You're only guessing."

"Whether or not I am the Shield, it's still my job to protect you and Mina. Don't go getting your feminist panties in a twist," he said as I began to sputter. "That's simply the way it is. I know Jack would agree."

"Of course he would, but that's entirely beside the point. I don't for one minute believe you're simply worried about Mina's safety. I just wish you would admit it and move on." I harped on this argument frequently.

"Weren't we talking about you wanting to return to the U.S.?" He deftly changed the subject. "I worry Luc will try to stop you, but I also don't see any continued value in you remaining in France unless you wish to make it your permanent home. No, I didn't think so." He smiled wryly as I shook my head.

"I need to go home, Rémy, but what does that mean for you? What does it mean for Mina?"

"Cherié, you don't need to worry—"

"No, Rémy!" I wheeled around to face him, grabbing his arms. "Just stop, okay? I'm tired of you doing that! I'm not a little girl any more. I need to make my own decisions, live my own life, and you need to live yours instead of following me around, trying to protect me! I'm so sick and tired of trying to live up to what some damn prophecy might or might not mean! Aren't you sick of it yet?

How long can you go on living like this? How long can you put off your own plans and dreams? I know you're in love with—"

"Don't say it!" He broke free of my hold and whirled away from me. "Please, don't say it," he begged, running his hands through his hair.

He sounded so miserable. I stepped forward and put my hand on his shoulder. "I'm sorry."

He turned and put his arms around me, resting his head atop mine. "I know. None of this is your fault, cherié."

"Yeah, well it's not yours, either. We deserve a life, Rémy."

"I agree. I just don't know how to make that happen." He kissed the top of my head and pulled away. "Let's go." He took my arm and led me toward the apartment.

***

I felt it as I reached for the doorknob of my apartment: the hair on the back of my neck raised and goose bumps appeared all over my arms. "Something's wrong." I pulled my hand back from the door.

"Get behind me." Rémy pushed me out of the way. Normally, I would take exception to this kind of manhandling, but I could sense something was terribly wrong inside the apartment. He reached into his back waistband and pulled out a handgun of some sort.

"Where did you get that?" I whispered furiously.

"Shh!" He pushed me against the wall and

reached for the doorknob. "Stay out here until I find out what's going on." The door was unlocked, which was unusual, and not like the ever-cautious Mina. Rémy pushed it open and entered the apartment, gun drawn. I heard him walk through the rooms calling for Mina, heard the bathroom and bedroom doors crashing open as he checked. He popped his head back out the door, saying, "It's clear. You can come in."

"Where's Mina?" I asked as I walked through our apartment, which showed clear signs of a struggle. He didn't answer and I walked back into the living room to find him seated on our couch, head in his hands. The entire apartment was buzzing with energy from the events that had occurred there earlier. I began moving through the apartment again, this time touching all the various pieces of furniture and surfaces, concentrating on what the energy remnants told me. I had learned this talent from all the times Grams had rifled through my stuff and had honed it in Cassie's office over the course of many months. Now was my chance to use it; it was one of the few powers I had that Rémy sucked at.

Mina had been sitting at the kitchen table, coding a website for the Giles family business. She walked over to the stove when the kettle whistled and began preparing a cup of tea. The knock on the door startled her, causing her to slop hot water on the counter. Ever cautious, she looked through the peephole before opening the door to sign for a UPS package. Her welcoming smile turned to fear as the package was shoved into her stomach and the fake UPS man, followed by Luc and two other men, pushed their way into the apartment. She hastily dropped the package and ran toward the bedrooms, grabbing her cell phone along the way. Her kitten screeched and high-tailed it to the back bedroom. The UPS impostor caught Mina as she reached the kitchen bar, grabbing her hair brutally and pulling her backward. She screamed, clawing and scratching at his face and arms as she tried desperately to get away. Her earring was ripped from her ear in the struggle. One of the other men came up behind them and injected something into her neck. She stopped struggling and sagged limply, unconscious.

"What do you see?" Rémy asked as he stood from the couch. "I can't reach—"

Stop! I yelled mentally. *Don't say anything!* I had seen what Luc and the other man was doing while the other two subdued Mina. *They bugged the apartment, Rémy. They're listening to us! Don't say anything! I don't know what they are hoping to hear, so be careful!* "Fergie!" I ran to Mina's bedroom and looked under her bed. Her kitten, a birthday gift from Rémy, was huddled in the far corner. He meowed pitifully when he saw me. I finally coaxed him out with a can of tuna and carried him to the kitchen, setting him on the counter to eat.

"I found her phone." Rémy came into the microscopic kitchen with Mina's phone, now sporting a shattered screen, as if it had been stomped. "I should have bought her a guard dog," he whispered as he roughed the kitten's head.

"It was Luc and several of his cronies." I told him everything I had seen as I moved through the apartment. I felt safe stating the obvious as Luc had witnessed demonstrations of my ability to touch objects and know what had happened or where they came from on numerous occasions. He would definitely know I would use it on this occasion. There was only one thing we had systematically kept secret from both Seer groups over the years: our ability to communicate mentally with each other. I suspected the listening devices had something to do with this. "Why would they take her, Rémy?"

He didn't answer as he bent down to examine something on the tile floor. He stood up holding a silver object in his palm.

"That's her earring!" I leaned closer to look. "Is that blood?" I slid down the cabinet as my knees gave out. Rémy sat down beside me. "They tore it out of her ear in the struggle. Poor Mina!"

Rémy stared at the bloody earring in his trembling palm. "I will find her," he vowed. "And I will kill Luc."

"She's not dead! We would know, wouldn't we?"

"I would know," he growled through clenched teeth.

My heart melted at his fierceness. I wove my arm through his and leaned against his shoulder. "You *are* in love with her, aren't you?"

He nodded miserably and leaned his head against

the cabinet. "And when I get her back, I'm going to tell her, finally, and beg her to forgive me for being such an ass. No prophecy in the world will keep me from her any longer!"

I said nothing, but rubbed his arm, hoping to soothe him. They had lived in denial of their love for each other for so long.

"I am beyond done with this!" Rémy said through clenched teeth. "That bastard wants to force something, to force us to do something?"

"You think that's why he took Mina?"

"I do. He's as tired of this cat and mouse game as we are."

"What is he trying to force?"

He shook his head. "I'm not sure." He stood, holding out his hand for me. "We need to get to Grandmére."

***

I packed Fergie into his kitty crate and we caught a taxi to Kate's estate. Rémy leaned forward, head in his hands. "I can't reach her." He sighed as he lifted his head, the most miserable expression I've ever seen on his face. "Nothing. She's never been able to block me out this completely. She must still be unconscious."

"Shh," I warned, noticing the driver glancing at us in the rearview mirror. *We have to be careful. Nobody can know about our abilities. It may be our only advantage.*

Do you think that could be why they planted the bugs? he asked.

I don't know, but I think we should keep it secret, now more than ever. I don't know what Luc expects to gain by bugging our apartment.

We remained silent the rest of the way, hesitant to speak of our secrets in front of the driver. Rémy texted his grandmother and she met us in the circular drive of her estate.

"Oh, my dears!" She pulled me into her arms. Her perfumed embrace caused my fragile emotions to crumble into tears.

"Kate, they took her! Mina's gone and we don't know where she is! They hurt her, Kate!" I sobbed against her shoulder.

Rémy paid the cab driver and joined us on the front steps. Kate set me aside gently and hugged her grandson. He remained stiff in her arms for a few seconds, but relented as she whispered to him in French. He put his arms around her, clutching her desperately. "I need to get her back, Grandmére," he said as he pulled away. My stomach clenched in sympathy as I watched him wipe his eyes.

"We will, Rémy," she said as she held his face in her hands. "I promise you we will." She let him go and ushered both of us inside. She led us into her private sitting room and asked André to bring a tea tray. Rémy eschewed the tea and went straight for the mini bar, pouring himself a healthy amount of amber liquid, which he downed quickly. Kate and I exchanged sympathetic, worried glances.

"I didn't protect her," he whispered to no one in particular.

"All right, Rémy. That's enough!" Kate's tone was stern. "We do not have time for that line of thought. We need to figure out what to do. Now come sit down and tell me exactly what happened."

He obeyed, but after a few minutes he was back to pacing in front of the bay windows, sipping another drink. I told Kate everything we had seen at the apartment and everything I had sensed. When I reached the end of my story and had finally answered all Kate's questions, I stalked across the room to Rémy and took the drink from his hand. "I need you sober, okay? So does Mina. We'll find her, Rémy. I swear we will."

He stood, glaring, before finally nodding and allowing me to lead him back to the sofa.

"Why don't you both rest here while I call the rest of the Conseil; they need to be informed." Kate bustled out.

"I need to call Fionnuala," I said. "God, what am I going to tell her?" Rémy sat beside me while I talked to the head of the Irish Seers. When I couldn't speak coherently through my tears, he took the phone and finished telling her what little we knew.

"She and Caoimhe will catch the next possible flight," he said as he handed the phone back to me. He fell back against the couch, throwing his arm over his face. "How did this happen? Why would Luc take Mina? What could he possibly hope to gain?"

"I don't know, Rémy. I would have thought he'd take you or me if he were going to take anyone. Can't we call the police? This is kidnapping!"

"I don't think so, at least not yet. She's an adult and has only been gone for a few hours. How would we explain how we know she's been taken?"

"How about the fact that our apartment is wrecked? I think it's pretty clear something bad happened there!" I was yelling, but couldn't bring myself to calm down.

"Yes, but how would we tell them we know who took her? How useful would it be for the police to be involved when we can't tell them anything about Luc?"

I hated that he had a point. "Yeah, I guess you're right," I said grudgingly. "Can you think of anywhere he might be keeping her? You've been tracking him for a year," I asked hopefully.

"I'm racking my brain, but none of the places I tracked him would be the kind of place he would need to keep a captive. I just don't know, cherié. I don't know what to say or think."

Poor Rémy! He was lost without Mina and I realized how much we had both come to rely on her quiet way of keeping us both calm. "She always knows exactly what to say, doesn't she? She always seems to know what we're feeling and how to make us feel better," I mused. "What?" I asked when I noticed he was staring at me intensely.

"You're right. I never thought of it that way." He flopped back against the sofa, lost in thought.

"I took her for granted," I whispered.

"So did I, cherié." He sat up and rubbed my shoulders. "So did I. But I will find her, and I will never take her for granted again," he vowed.

"Rémy, Ally!" Geneviève rushed in, followed by her husband, Arnaud. *"Nous sommes venus tout de suite après avoir entendu les nouvelles! Qu'est-ce*

qu'on peut faire pour trouver notre douce Mina?"
She threw herself in her cousin's arms rather
dramatically.

"Thank you, Geneviève." He met Arnaud's
exasperated look over her shoulder. "I don't quite
know what to do, to be honest. I want to rush out
and look for her, but I have absolutely no idea
where to start."

"Come, *mon petit*." Arnaud gently disengaged
his wife from Rémy. "You don't need to get
yourself too excited. Why don't you sit over here?"
He led her over to the couch as Rémy and I
exchanged bemused glances.

"Oh, Arnaud, stop fussing! I'm fine! I hope
you're not going to be this overprotective for the
next six months."

Six months? Why would he…oh! "Geneviève!
Oh, my goodness! You're pregnant?" I exclaimed.

"Oui, but I was going to wait to tell you until
after we find Mina," she explained while giving
Arnaud a dirty look.

"That's wonderful! Congratulations! A baby!
Oh, Geneviève!" I pulled her in for a hug while
Rémy slapped Arnaud—who was unsuccessfully
trying to smother a smug grin—on the back.

"Well, I guess the secret is out," she said.

"I'm glad," I stated. "We needed some good
news today."

We filled them in on the details of what little we
knew about Mina's disappearance and then had to
turn around and repeat the story two more times as
the rest of the Conseil appeared in waves over the
next hour. I was emotionally exhausted and a text

from Jack was all the reason I needed to excuse myself to the hallway so I could call him. It was 11:00 a.m. in Albuquerque, so I figured he must be on a lunch break from classes. He had finals this week and would graduate in two weeks with his bachelor's degree. With me gone, he had taken a heavy load both semesters, saying he had nothing better to do than study. Since he still had a year left on his scholarship, the army had agreed to let him continue on to a master's program at the university before he began his active duty.

"Ally, hon, what's up? You never answered my text."

"I'm so sorry, Jack. They took Mina! Luc took her!"

"Okay, slow down, sweetheart. Tell me what happened."

The sound of his voice washed over me, calming me and allowing me to concentrate for the first time since I had touched the doorknob of my apartment. I told him about Mina's disappearance and how I sensed what had happened in the apartment. "She was so scared, Jack! I can't imagine what she's going through right now!"

"Yes, you can, querida. You know exactly what she's going through, and you know she can get through this, just like you did. Now tell me what you and Rémy are planning."

"That's just it, Jack. We don't have a plan. We don't know where to start. We don't know why Luc would take her or what he could possibly hope to gain by taking Mina."

"It sounds like he's desperate and is trying to

start something," he said.

"That's what Rémy thinks, but we have no idea what he's trying to start. Jack, I was ready to come home, but now—"

"Ally, I don't want you anywhere near that crazy bastard! Come home. Let Rémy and the rest of them find Mina."

I smiled sadly, because we both knew that wouldn't happen. "I love you, Jack."

"I love you, too. Sweetheart, you believe that, don't you? In your email you said 'I hope you still love me.' What's that about?"

I shook my head and then realized he couldn't see me. "I'm sorry, Jack. I know you do, I just—"

"You just what? Come on, hon. We've been through too much for you to doubt me."

"I don't doubt you, Jack." I sniffed.

"Jesus, Ally. Don't cry. Please."

"I'm not," I cried. Then I laughed. Of course I was crying. "God, Jack. I'm a mess."

"I can be there tomorrow, next day at the latest. I need to be there," he said firmly.

I sniffed again and pulled myself together. "No. Absolutely not. I'm fine. I promise. This isn't about me, anyway. It's about Mina."

"I want to be there."

"I know, but you need to finish school. We're going to find Mina and then I'm coming home. Please stay there, Jack. It will just be one more thing for me to worry about. And I know you love me. I'm just being my usual crazy, stressed self. I'm okay, I promise."

I heard him sigh and I could picture him

scrubbing his hands over his face. "Okay. I know I can't just forget everything here and fly over there. Please be careful. Please, Ally."

"There's nothing to be careful about yet. I'm just lounging around the estate." I promised to keep him informed about our plans and continued to talk him out of blowing off the rest of his finals to fly over to help.

After picking at the dinner Kate ordered for everyone, I retired to the guest bedroom I always used. Everyone was staying at the estate until we found Mina. I had to believe that was possible.

Chapter Two

"There are some villainies that bring no gain. For by dishonesty the few may thrive, The many come to ruin and disgrace."
—Sophocles, Antigone

Day 2

Rémy let himself in the back door as I entered the kitchen early the next morning. He was wearing the same clothes from the day before, now rumpled. He had obviously been up all night and looked exhausted and depressed. He tossed his keys on the table as he sunk into a chair, staring straight ahead, his gaze unfocused. I poured a cup of coffee and set it in front of him, prepared the way he liked it: one sugar and lots of milk.

He glanced up at me in surprise. "Merci, Ally. I didn't see you. Why are you up so early? It's not even six o'clock."

"I woke up and couldn't get back to sleep. My brain won't stop churning," I said with a sigh. "You want some breakfast?"

"No, but I'll eat anyway." He stood and began gathering items from the refrigerator. "Is an omelet all right with you?"

"I was offering to make breakfast for you," I said, exasperated.

"I know, cherié, but since I don't care for cold cereal, I'd better handle the cooking."

"Pig," I said fondly. We had been over this too many times for me to be offended.

"Princess," he responded, cracking eggs in a bowl and beating them.

Within minutes he set a beautiful omelet in front of me and one for himself at the opposite side of the table. It was delicious, but neither of us had much of an appetite. We forced ourselves to eat half our breakfast while Rémy filled me in on his nocturnal activities.

"I couldn't sleep, so I decided to check out Luc's apartment in town." At my raised eyebrows he shook his head. "Nothing. There are new tenants."

"So, what did you do for the rest of the night?"

"Drove around aimlessly, trying to think of somewhere I could search." He sighed. "I have no idea where she could be."

My heart melted at his forlorn tone. "Why don't you get some sleep? I promise I'll wake you the second we hear anything."

"I'll sleep when she comes home." He stood and carried our plates to the sink. "I need to take a shower and shave before I go out again."

"At least let me come with you."

He smiled tiredly and nodded. "Of course. Can

you be ready in half an hour?"

We drove all over Rouen, looking in alleyways and up and down every street, but saw no trace of Mina. Try as we might, neither of us could get the slightest hint of a mental connection with her; either she was unconscious or purposely blocking us. We both refused to consider any other reason for her lack of connection. We finally gave up around 3 p.m. and headed back to Kate's, disheartened and exhausted. We entered the living room to find Fionnuala and Caoimhe had arrived in our absence. Caoimhe opened her arms to me and I reveled in a few moments of unleashed emotions as she rubbed her hands up and down my back and whispered comforting nonsense. Fionnuala was all business, demanding to know what we had done and where we had looked.

"And there's been no word? No demands from her kidnappers?" At all our blank looks and negative head shakes, she stood abruptly and stalked to the window. "What do you know about this Luc? I think I met him once, didn't I?"

"Yes, when you brought Mina here for the first time," I replied.

"You have been chasing him for the past year, haven't you, young man? You have found nothing?" She rounded on Rémy angrily.

"Fionnuala!" I exclaimed, appalled at her accusing tone.

"No, Ally," Rémy said. "It's perfectly all right. I have been chasing him for the past year, and I have found very little. Luc and his group have always been one step ahead of me, taunting me, and now I let them take Mina."

"You didn't 'let' them take her! You can't blame yourself for this, Rémy!" I tried to keep from yelling.

"Yes, I can. I do. It's my job to protect you both and I failed. I will never forgive myself," he said matter-of-factly.

"Rémy, tell them what we know about Les Dépaysés," Kate ordered.

"About what?" Caoimhe asked.

"Les Dépaysés. It means to be without country or homeland. Basically dispossessed. It is what Luc is calling the group of followers he has been gathering. He has spent the past several years traveling all over Europe searching for unknown Seers that might be sympathetic to his message," Rémy explained.

"And what is his message?" Fionnuala demanded.

"That Seers should rise up and take over the world. Or at least France. Luc has political aspirations, apparently. I have heard he has been searching for children lately. He hopes to find others with powers like Ally, Mina, and myself."

"What could he possibly want with our sweet Mina?" Caoimhe wondered aloud.

"We think he may be trying to force some sort of action or confrontation," Kate said. "He may be as tired of the chase as we are. I fear this could be his first step. I am very much afraid of what else he plans."

"It doesn't matter what else he plans or what his next step is. Right now all I care about is getting

Mina back!" Fionnuala yelled into her sister's face.

Kate, to her credit, didn't react negatively. She simply put her arms around Fionnuala and pulled her close. Fionnuala resisted for a few seconds, then allowed herself to be comforted.

Rémy motioned for me to follow him and we exited, leaving the sisters alone.

***

Day 3

No word from Mina or Luc. We spent most of the day pacing the floors at the estate, hoping to hear something. Anything. Geneviève paced and worried with us until Arnaud made her lie down, telling her she needed to take care of herself for the baby's sake. I had no such luck getting Rémy to rest. I had never seen him so disheveled before: he had dark circles under his eyes, a day's beard growth, and he wore a rumpled t-shirt and jeans. There was nothing left of the urbane young businessman he normally presented to the world; he was reduced to the raw material of a man desperately trying to find the woman he loved. After picking at his lunch, he grabbed his car keys and stormed out.

"Where are we going?" I asked as I climbed in the passenger seat and fastened my seat belt.

"I have no idea. You probably shouldn't come with me."

"Oh, I definitely should, if for no other reason than to make sure you keep your speed to a semi-reasonable level so you don't wrap your car around a tree or something. I would hate to have bad news for Mina when we get her back."

He chuckled briefly and mirthlessly. "All right. Point taken." He drove for hours, heading basically north through an endless parade of small towns including Bois-Guillame, Isneauville, and Quincampoix before circling back. We stopped multiple times to show her picture and ask if anyone had seen her. No one had. It was as if she had disappeared into thin air.

"Your stomach is hurting, cherié?" Rémy glanced over as I was clutching my stomach.

"I'm fine." I forced myself to clasp my hands in my lap and ignore the pain shooting through my gut.

"Let's stop by your apartment so you can get your medicine."

He wandered through the apartment as I went to the bathroom to gather the prescription pain medication that made my life bearable when I had an attack. I took the opportunity to pack a bag since I had left with only the clothes on my back and then walked to the living room, expecting to find Rémy. He wasn't there and I found him sitting on Mina's bed, holding a stuffed animal he had won for her at a local fair a few weeks ago.

"She kept this? I don't even know what it's supposed to be."

"I think it's a bear of some sort. She loves it." I sat beside him and reached for the toy.

"It's hideous," he scoffed.

"But you gave it to her, and she loves you," I

explained patiently. Really, guys could be so dense sometimes. I felt horrible for the uncharitable thought when he inhaled sharply and lowered his head to his hands, his back heaving as he tried to control his sobs. I had never seen him cry and it floored me. "Hey, come on." I put my arm around him. "We're going to get her back. We have to. Now, let's head back so you can get some sleep. You're so exhausted you can't even think straight."

He pulled himself together quickly and insisted on helping me pack a bag of Mina's things so she would have fresh clothes when we found her.

"Thank you, Ally," he said as he drove, staring out the windshield.

"For what?"

"For staying so positive. I'm tired and I tend to get negative when I haven't slept. I'm afraid that if I fall asleep something will happen."

"I promise to wake you up the second we hear anything, okay? I swear I won't let you sleep through anything important."

I had to repeat my assurances when we got back to the estate and it took Geneviève's assistance to bully him into sleeping for a few hours. I spent an hour talking to Jack on FaceTime, catching him up on what had happened and what we had done.

"How are you holding up, querida?" he asked softly.

"I'm okay, Jack. This isn't about me."

"I know. I also know you probably aren't taking care of yourself. How is your stomach?"

I sighed. "Not great, but I got my medicine and I'm doing a little better. How are your finals going?" I needed to talk about something normal, if even for just a few minutes.

He seemed to understand my need, as he always did. "Oh, they're going okay, I guess. I turn my senior design project in on Wednesday and then I have a paper for that friggin' U.S. History class I had to take. God, a required social studies elective my senior year? What the hell?"

I laughed, glad to talk about his life for a while. "Poor Jack! What are you writing your paper on?"

"I don't know. Something about the effect of big business after the Civil War or some crap like that."

"That sounds interesting," I offered.

"No, it doesn't. It's incredibly boring. I hate essays."

I remembered how much he had hated them when we were in high school, frequently begging me to help him figure out what to write. We were so opposite in our academic pursuits: he would rather do a set of math problems or design something while I would rather write a paper or read a book. He loved to read, but only when he chose the book. The second it was required, he lost all interest. "Well, why don't you send it to me? I'll help you polish it."

"No, sweetheart. You have your hands full trying to find Mina. The last thing you need is to worry about my stupid history final."

"Actually, it would be great to have something to focus on besides this futile search through Normandy. Please send it. I promise to ignore it if something happens with Mina."

"Okay, but don't worry if you don't get around

to it. Ally, when are you coming home? I need you here," he admitted quietly.

"I don't know, Jack. I'm so ready to be home and I will be so upset if I miss your graduation, but I can't leave until we find Mina."

"This sucks so bad. I want to help. I can't stand this!"

"I know, I know. I'm going crazy too. God, Jack, you should see Rémy. He's a mess. If we don't find her, I don't know—"

"We're going to find her. Don't give up, babe. Listen, if nothing happens by this weekend I'm going to come over there and help you look. I'll finish with my finals Friday and can be on a plane by Saturday at the latest."

"Jack, your graduation is the next weekend! You can't miss that!"

"I couldn't care less about walking for graduation. I'm just doing it for Trina and Manny's sake. Finding Mina is way more important," he stated firmly.

"Okay, okay. Hopefully you won't have to do that. I pray we can find her in the next couple of days and I can go home." We signed off and I went to bed, although I only managed to toss and turn for a few hours. I finally gave up and headed to the kitchen to make some tea, stopping to check on Rémy as I passed his bedroom. He was still fast asleep, thank goodness.

I found Kate and Phillipe in the kitchen.

"Couldn't you sleep, Ally love?" Kate asked as Phillipe pulled out a chair for me.

"Not really. I spent more time tossing and

turning than sleeping, so I thought I'd try some herbal tea. Rémy's still asleep, though."

"Yes. I checked on him a little while ago, as well. Sit down and I'll make you some tea and toast. Phillipe and I were just about to have some."

Within a few minutes I had tea and buttery, delicious toast in front of me. "Have you heard anything else, Kate?" I asked hopefully.

"I did talk to a friend of mine who said she has heard rumors of Luc in London recently."

"What would he be doing in England?" I wondered aloud.

"I suspect he is trying to recruit Seers who do not have a close affiliation with any particular council," Kate said.

"Oh, great. That's all we need. How many Seers are there, anyway?"

"We don't have any way of truly knowing, Ally," Phillipe piped in. "There is no way of knowing or keeping track. That is one of the things Luc has always bemoaned. He feels we should be making some sort of effort to count and categorize Seers all over the world."

"For what purpose? Aren't we supposed to stay kind of on the down-low?" They both gave me blank looks, apparently not understanding my American idiom. "You know, stay unknown?"

"Ah, oui." Phillipe nodded. "Both our Conseil and our Irish counterparts believe Seers should indeed be extremely discreet about our powers. Most Seers these days have such limited powers that it doesn't present much of a problem, but you and Rémy are changing that."

"What about Mina?"

They exchanged a look I didn't like at all. "What? Why did you look at each other like that? She's just as powerful as Rémy and me! Wait," I said as they refused to meet my gaze. "Oh my God! You don't think we're going to find her!" I stood up so fast I knocked my chair over.

"No, Ally! That's not it," Kate rushed to assure me. "I absolutely believe we will find her. We must, for Rémy's sake. He is very much in love with her, you know."

"I know. She loves him too."

"Does she? I've worried that it was all on Rémy's part."

"Believe me, she loves him. I don't know why they can't work it out, why they both keep holding back. So, what are you concerned about? Beyond finding her, I mean."

"It's just that we don't really know very much about her gifts, do we? Although you have been exceptionally circumspect about it, I suspect she shares your mental communication abilities. But is that it? Has she shared anything else with you?"

I shook my head. "No. She has crazy mind reading skills, maybe even better than Rémy. They're both way better than me, but I don't think Mina knows what else she can do. Can powers show up at her age?"

"You make it sound like she's in her dotage!" Kate exclaimed as she carried my plate to the sink. "She's only 22 years old, for heaven's sake! But to answer your question, I don't know. Our gifts usually manifest by the time we are 18, but the rules certainly seem to be changing lately. I truly don't know, Ally. Anything is possible at this point."

***

Day 4

My phone dinged a message alert while I was blow-drying my hair after a much-needed shower. It was an unknown number, but the first words had me fumbling to punch in my PIN and read.

Its Mina. Im ok. Cant use our reg way communicate. Dont. Watched. Call soon. Tell Remy.

I raced to Rémy's bedroom and entered without even knocking. He was still asleep, lying on his stomach with his hands under his pillow. It looked like he had taken a shower but hadn't shaved; he was wearing a robe and hadn't bothered to get under the covers. "Rémy." I shook his shoulder lightly, hating to wake him but knowing he would never forgive me if I didn't. "Rémy, I got a text from Mina. She's okay. She's going to call soon." He sat up instantly, rubbing his hand over his face.

"Let me see."

I handed him my phone. "It's pretty disjointed, but I think she's warning us to stop trying to send her mental messages for some reason. I don't understand."

"No, neither do I. What does she mean by 'watched'?"

"I don't know. Why don't you—" My phone ringing interrupted me. "Mina?" I nearly shouted.

"Ally!" she cried on the other end.

Rémy grabbed it from me. "Mina? Where are you? Are you all right?"

"Speaker! Put it on speaker, Rémy!" I hissed while trying to grab it from him. He complied and held it in front of us. "Mina, darling, where are you?"

"I…I don't know. I woke up on the beach a little while ago. I don't know where I am. I'm not, um, thinking very clearly right now." She sniffed, obviously trying not to cry.

"Mina, whose phone are you using?" Rémy asked patiently. We had found hers smashed in our apartment.

"A really nice lady found me and let me use her phone," she whimpered.

"Let me talk to her, please." He continued to soothe her softly. He began a conversation in rapid French a few seconds later, but I was too distracted to concentrate enough to understand it. "Mina, we're coming to get you," he told her when she was back on the phone. "Ally and I are coming to get you. Madame Meunieur is going to take you to her home. You can rest there and wait for us. You'll be safe there, Mina, I promise. We'll be there soon."

"Mina, honey, we'll be there really soon, okay?" I added.

"Okay." I could hear her sniffling. "Remember what I told you, Ally. He's watching." She hung up.

Rémy was wrenching dresser drawers open and throwing clothes on the bed. He ripped his robe off;

I winced and closed my eyes when I realized he was commando underneath. "Geez, Rémy!"

"Sorry, cherié." He didn't sound sorry. "Can you be ready to go in five minutes? I don't want to waste any time."

"Of course. Where are we going? Where is she?"

"In Brest. A town called Le Conquet. Can you bring her bag?"

Less than fifteen minutes later we were on the road. It had taken some time to tell Kate and Phillipe where we were going and promise to keep in touch. Kate filled a thermos with coffee and threw together a few sandwiches for our trip, knowing Rémy wouldn't be willing to stop until we had reached Mina.

"How far away is Le Conquet?" I asked as I poured him a cup of coffee.

He finished programming the GPS and took the cup with a grateful smile. "About four hundred and thirty kilometers. It will take about five and a half hours to get there," he stated grimly.

"What did the woman who found her say?" At his confused look I explained. "You were speaking so fast and I couldn't concentrate."

He nodded. "She was walking her dog early this morning and found Mina on the beach. She wasn't sure if she was dead, drunk, or just sleeping. I'm sure she was drugged and left on the beach. Bastard!"

I couldn't disagree with him so I said nothing. I sent Jack a text letting him know what was going on and that I would call as soon as I could. We drove in silence most of the way and I actually fell asleep for nearly an hour, waking as the car slowed. "Are we there?" I asked sleepily.

"Just about." He drove through the small fishing village, pulling up in front of a charming stone cottage with the beach visible in the background. I followed him to the front door and stood to the side while he knocked firmly. A middle-aged woman opened it and Rémy introduced us. Madame Meunieur invited us in, motioning for us to be quiet, as the young lady had finally fallen asleep. She led us to the back room where Mina was asleep on the sofa, covered with a knitted afghan. Rémy knelt in front of her and gently pushed her black hair out of her eyes. "Mina? Wake up, please."

She blinked, trying to focus. "Rémy? Oh!" She sat up and threw herself into his arms. He managed to pull himself onto the couch without ever letting her go and they held each other tightly for endless seconds before he pulled back and kissed her.

"Are you all right?" he asked as he pulled her against him again.

"I am now," she said.

"God, Mina," he groaned and kissed her again. "I'm so sorry! I didn't protect you. I let him take you," he whispered against her lips. "I'm so sorry."

"Shh." She framed his face, running her hands across his scruffy, unshaven cheeks. "I'm all right. It wasn't your fault."

"I love you, Mina. I've loved you for so long. I can't pretend any longer. I don't care about the prophecy. Maybe you don't love—"

She kissed him before he could finish his ridiculous statement. "Of course I love you. How could you not know that?" They kissed for another long moment before Mina noticed me. "Ally!" She extricated herself from Rémy's arms and crossed the room to hug me.

"I was so worried about you!" We pulled back and smiled at the tears in each other's eyes. "Are you really okay?"

"Yes." She nodded. "I've been drugged a lot over the past few days and my head is killing me, but I'm okay."

We spent a few minutes thanking Elysse Meunieur for her help and hospitality. Rémy tried to pay her something for her trouble, but she politely, yet firmly refused. She recommended a good hotel in town where we could get a decent meal and some much-needed rest before driving back to Rouen the next morning. I gladly surrendered the front seat to Mina and called Kate while Rémy drove to the center of town. I texted Jack, told him that Mina was safe, and promised to call him later. Rémy pulled the car in front of the Pointe Ste Barbe hotel and guided us to the front desk, where he reserved two rooms: one for himself and one for Mina and me. A few minutes later we stood in front of our rooms and he presented Mina and me with our room keys. He seemed adorably flummoxed when Mina simply shook her head and stated that she would be staying with him in his room. I smiled wryly and let myself into my now private room. Rémy was still speechless, gaping like a fish, so Mina and I arranged for the three of us to meet in the restaurant downstairs for dinner in an hour—as soon as she had time to shower and change clothes. I offered to acquire some aspirin for her throbbing headache and headed out to find a pharmacy as soon as I dropped my bag in my room. After I returned from my errand of mercy, I called Jack and talked to him until it was time to meet in the restaurant. He was relieved we had found her and wanted to know how soon I would be home. I told him I planned to be home within a few days at the most, come hell or high water.

Mina looked refreshed but still pale as we sat down for dinner. She gratefully swallowed the aspirin and nibbled some bread while we waited for our meals to be delivered. I noticed that she and Rémy were loath to let go of each other's hand, even to eat. I was happy for them; it was about damn time they figured out they were crazy about each other.

"Mina, what happened? I know what happened at the apartment, but tell us what else happened. Where did Luc take you? Why?" I buttered a piece of bread as I asked, suddenly ravenous.

"I don't know where he took me. He kept me drugged most of the time. Shh." She leaned in to kiss Rémy as he growled. "I might have an idea *why* he took me, however." She paused as the waiter stopped by to refill our water glasses, then leaned in to whisper, "He has someone like Bridget who can read minds with a touch. He never let go of me until last night when they dropped me at the beach. That's why I couldn't contact you. I had to block you both out as hard as I could. I'm sorry. I knew you'd be worried, but I couldn't let them know about our connection. Luc suspects, but he can't be sure."

"Yes." Rémy nodded. "Ally figured that out, as well. She saw that he planted listening devices in your apartment. And you said he's watching us?"

Mina nodded. "I overheard them discussing it. They overestimated how long I would be unconscious and underestimated my comprehension of French." She had worked diligently over the past year to learn French, insisting we speak it exclusively at the apartment. It had annoyed me greatly at the time, but I was extremely grateful for it now.

"So, Luc suspects we have the ability to speak to each other with only our minds and he's watching us. Did you hear anything else?" Rémy asked as he put his arm around her.

"He's hoping this whole episode will cause some kind of reaction, something to do with the prophecy. I don't know what." She shook her head and reached for more water. "I'm so thirsty."

"It's the drugs they gave you," Rémy said as he kissed her hair. "I really need to kill that bastard."

"No, Rémy! Stay away from him! He's dangerous!"

"Okay, love. Shh. We don't have to talk about it right now." He wiped the tears beginning to streak down her cheeks and kissed her. "Let's just focus on the fact that we're here together." They kissed again, rather passionately, finally drawing apart when the waiter delivered our meals.

I was so happy for them that I didn't feel terribly *de trop,* but it did make me miss Jack and I must admit to feeling just a wee bit sorry for myself as I watched them. Sigh. Oh well, I would be seeing him soon. Mina was back safe and sound, so I could focus on going home.

***

They were late for breakfast. I was actually surprised they showed up at all, to be honest. I had slept with my headphones on so as to block out any possible extraneous noises from the adjoining room. But they finally appeared, Mina appearing radiant and Rémy looking smug, as I was drinking a celebratory cup of coffee rather than my usual herbal tea.

"Good morning, lovebirds. I figured I wouldn't see you two until at least lunchtime."

Mina blushed, but Rémy just laughed. "Yes, well, we need to get back to Rouen as soon as possible."

"What's the rush?" I asked.

"First, I need to take my fiancée shopping for an engagement ring."

"What? Oh my gosh! Congratulations!" I pushed my chair back and hugged Mina. "I'm so happy for you! Wow that was fast."

"Not really," Rémy said as he hugged me. "I have loved this woman for three years. I was simply too much of an idiot to do anything about it. I'm not wasting anymore time." He put his arm around Mina's waist. "I'm going to marry her as soon as we are able to set up the ceremony."

I fumbled on the table for a napkin to wipe away the tears that were streaking down my cheeks.

"Here, cherié." He handed me his handkerchief. "There's no need to cry."

"Shut up. I'm happy, that's all. Finally, something good is happening for us."

"It is," he agreed. "I think it's long past time we started calling the shots. I've had it with waiting for the prophecy to reveal what it truly means and I'm sick to death of chasing Luc all over Western Europe. He wants something to happen. He took Mina to try and make it happen, so I say we oblige the bastard."

"What do you mean?" I asked.

"He is bound and determined to force the new Oracle to appear, right?" Both Mina and I nodded. "Well, let's give him what he wants. Mina says he's watching us, so let's give him something worth watching. Let's give him an ascension."

Chapter Three

"Still the same rough winds, the wild passion raging through the girl."
—Sophocles, Antigone

Back at the estate, we had to spend a few hours letting the Conseil members as well as Fionnuala and Caoimhe hug and make a huge fuss over Mina. Rémy and I watched good-naturedly, answering questions about how we found her and dodging questions about our plans for the near future. Rémy finally brought the questions to a halt by standing and announcing that his fiancée needed a good meal and then a nap. This had the desired effect of immediately turning everyone's thoughts away from what would happen next as the women all rushed to hug Mina and the men pounded Rémy on the back and teased him about having to give up his free-wheeling bachelor ways. André, the majordomo, interrupted to announce lunch, but dropped his formal manners for a moment to congratulate Rémy, whom he had known since he was in diapers.

"Madame Giles, you will, of course, wish me to chill some champagne for lunch?" he addressed Kate as he left the room.

"Thank you, André." She nodded regally. "That will be wonderful. Let's have the Belle Epoque 2004, shall we? Mina will love it."

"She certainly should," Rémy muttered under his breath as he ushered both of us to the dining room.

"Let me guess: it's hideously expensive?" I asked.

"Oui. About 300 euros a bottle."

"Oh, Rémy! That's too much! Tell her no, please," Mina said.

"No, *mignonne*." He pulled her close and kissed her hair. "We must let her make a fuss. She's simply relieved someone has finally agreed to take me off her hands. I think she was beginning to despair of it ever happening."

"You are ridiculous." She laughed as she rounded on him. "You are a very sweet man, Monsieur Giles. I am definitely the lucky one in this whole arrangement." She kissed his cheek sweetly.

"*Mais no*." He framed her face with his hands. "I am the lucky one." Then they were kissing. Again. Sigh.

I rolled my eyes and left them to it while I continued on to the dining room. The newly engaged couple finally appeared and a lively lunch ensued during which the topic never strayed far from wedding plans. I started having flashbacks to my mother's wedding and could swear I felt hives beginning to break out all over my body. Rémy indulged his grandmother, but I suspected he would step in and keep her from turning his wedding into the spectacle it was quickly becoming. We toasted the happy couple with the expensive champagne. As the fruity pink bubbles tickled my tongue I looked around the table and estimated that each luncheon guest was imbibing approximately 40 euros worth of alcohol. Random, yet interesting thought.

Rémy managed to convince Mina to lie down for a short nap after lunch; she was not yet fully recovered from her ordeal and I knew she hadn't had a full night's sleep. Ahem. She would be sleeping in her old bedroom, where she slept whenever we stayed at the estate, but I suspected there would be some surreptitious nocturnal field trips across the hall to Rémy's room. Not that I was jealous. Not at all. Really.

Rémy and I met Kate and Phillipe in their private drawing room.

"Now, what is it you are planning, Rémy, and how can we help?" Kate asked once we had seated ourselves.

"Nothing gets by you, does it, Grandmére?" he said with a chuckle.

"No," she replied archly. "You very neatly turned the conversation earlier, but I know how your mind works. Now, spill."

"First, I have a question. How did you become the Oracle, Grandmére? How did it happen? What was it like? How did you know?"

"That's a good bit more than one question." She raised an eyebrow. "I trust this has to do with your plans?" At his nod, she continued. "I'll never forget that day. I was barely 18 years old and we were living in Belclare, not too far from Galway. Fionnuala was 20 and we were planning to move to the city soon and room together. There were no jobs in our village, so we were going to move to the big city and take it by storm." She smiled mistily, staring past us, momentarily transported back to Ireland in the late 1960s. "Anyway, we were baking bread in Mother's tiny kitchen one afternoon when I got all tingly and felt faint. I sat down and put my head on the table, thinking I was getting sick. Fionnuala said that I had a glow around me, but I couldn't see it. I started speaking. It was my first prophecy. I didn't know what I said, but Mother and Fionnuala wrote it down."

"What did it say?" I asked.

"Phillipe, darling, would you get the book, please?" Kate asked.

"Of course." He rose from the sofa and slipped into their bedroom through the adjoining door. He returned momentarily, carrying a scrapbook of sorts, which he handed to Kate.

She opened it and flipped a few pages in. "This is where we keep a copy of all the prophecies since I have been the Oracle. Ah, here we go: my first prophecy. 'The world of Seers is changing. The old ways are passing away. Many will arise in the days to come, but not all for the good.' That's it." She closed the book.

"So, the prophecies have always been maddeningly vague, huh? Well, shit, Kate! That sucks!" I exclaimed.

The other three laughed as I dropped my head to

my hands. I had to join them as I realized the futility of our position.

Kate gathered her wits first. "Now, what is it you are planning, Rémy?"

"When Mina was being held, she overheard some of the things Luc is planning. One of the reasons he took her was to try and force something to happen. I think something should happen, soon, before too much time has passed. I think we should stage Ally's ascension."

Kate gasped and stood to pace. "Hmm, yes. Perhaps. We might be able to make it work if Ally can control her power enough to make it appear authentic," she mused. "We'll have to practice—a lot—and we'll need a convincing first prophecy, but it could work."

"I can work on that," Phillipe said. "You will need to work with Ally, Mina, and Rémy. It will need to involve all three to be really convincing after what happened the first time they all touched." He referred to the time when we first met Mina; we had blown all the windows out in Kate's living room when the three of us touched for the first time. Since then we had been very careful to harness our thoughts and energy whenever we were all together.

"Mina and I will do whatever it takes," Rémy began.

"Wait a minute!" I yelled. "What are you all taking about? How can we have an ascension or a new Oracle while the old one is still alive?"

"Old one?" Kate said. "I believe I'm offended."

"Sorry. That's not what I meant. I meant while the *present* Oracle is still alive. I didn't mean to call you old."

"That's all right, dear. I suppose I am old to you. As to your objection, there is no hard and fast rule when it comes to Oracle ascension. There have been stories of when more than one Oracle was living at the same time. This could work, Ally. It may be our best hope."

"Our best hope for what? What do we gain if he thinks I'm the Oracle?"

"We gain the upper hand, cherié!" Rémy exclaimed as he grabbed me by the shoulders, forcing me to look him in the eyes. "Luc has been trying to gain control over you before you become the Oracle. This latest episode, kidnapping Mina, tipped his hand, though. He has become desperate and careless."

I pushed his hands away and ran my hands through my hair. "I still don't see what the advantage is if he thinks I'm the Oracle."

"The advantage is in what your prophecies will be," Phillipe broke in. "We will have complete control and can make it very unattractive for him to think about trying to control you any longer."

"I don't think I can pull it off," I whispered. "I'm a terrible liar and an even worse actress."

"Don't worry, cherié. I am an excellent liar. I will help you."

"That is nothing to brag about, Rémy," Kate said archly. "We will practice, Ally. You can do this. You are one of the strongest young women I have ever met. I know you can do this."

"Okay." I nodded, swayed by her belief in me. "Thanks, Kate. I'll try, I guess." At least it would be action of some sort.

"That's the spirit!" Rémy said. "Now, if you will excuse me I will go see if my fiancée is awake. I would like to take her into town and buy her an engagement ring." He left the room, humming under his breath.

I half-smiled as I watched him go, happy that two of my best friends had found happiness. I turned back to Kate in time to notice her wiping away a tear. "Oh, Kate. Don't cry. He's so happy."

"I know. That's why I'm crying. He's waited so long. They both have! I'm so sorry I was a big part of why they felt they had to wait. I should never have tried to push you and Rémy together. Can you forgive me, Ally?"

"Of course, Kate. Don't worry. Rémy and I had no intention of ever letting you push us together. It's nice to see him so happy, isn't it?"

"Oh, yes, it is." She patted my arm. "Your time will come, Ally. Try to be patient."

I smiled, but couldn't hold it. "Tell me the rest of the story, Kate. Please."

"The rest?"

"What happened after you had the prophecy? How did you get your happy ending?" My own seemed like such a distant dream; I needed to hear about someone else's.

"Oh, sweetie, what is a happy ending? I certainly don't feel like I've reached the end of anything, although you think I'm all dried up."

"I don't think—" I began.

"Hush. It's all right. I was the same way when I was your age. So, you want to know the rest of the story? Well, my mother realized right away what had happened and notified the Seer Council and I was whisked off to Galway post haste. Fionnuala went with me and was soon embroiled in all the politics of the Council. I was terribly bored with it all and had to be coaxed every time to attend to my training, very much like another young Oracle I know."

I felt the heat rise in my face, but defended myself. "We don't know for sure that I am the next Oracle. You knew before you had to train."

"Point taken. Anyway, I was 18 and in the big city for the first time and wanted to be anywhere except in a stuffy basement, training to develop my powers. Then, a handsome young man began working at the nearby pub. He was 21, incredibly sexy, and French."

"Phillipe?" I asked.

"Yes. The Conseil had sent him to see if the rumors of a new Oracle were true. He didn't tell me who he really was, of course. He was supposed to be spying on me, but it didn't quite work out that way."

"Because you fell in love."

"Madly. And stupidly." She laughed. "I knew better than to tell anyone. I was the Oracle, after all. I was supposed to be above petty things like love."

"Now you sound like Luc," I scoffed.

She shrugged. "They had the best intentions, but they put the needs of the Council above the desires of an impetuous young woman. Phillipe finally confessed who he was and asked me to marry him. I told Fionnuala and she told the Council."

"Ouch." I winced.

"Yes. They immediately forbade me from seeing him. I immediately disobeyed, of course."

"Of course." I nodded. "You eloped with him, didn't you? You left your family and ran off to France with Phillipe."

"Yes, I did. I had to make a choice and I chose Phillipe. He became my family. I was in love and I was pregnant." She looked at me. "Are you shocked?"

"No." I hastened to assure her. She raised her eyebrows. "Well, maybe a little surprised, but I'm not judging. That was Rémy's father, wasn't it?"

"Yes, Anton. So, I guess that is what you would call my 'happy ever after,' although I'm certainly not finished with my story yet."

I thought for a moment. "Do you have any regrets?"

"No." She smiled and shook her head. "Life is too short for regrets. I have a wonderful husband, an amazing son, and a grandson I adore. I could wish Fionnuala and I hadn't been estranged for so long, but it was a price I had to pay."

"Thanks for telling me, Kate. I think you're a really strong lady."

"That makes two of us. Let's start practicing for the big event, shall we?"

We spent several hours trying to manipulate my defensive power into a glow of some sort. I was finally able to manufacture a weak glow, but it remained blue no matter what I tried.

"All right, Ally. Let's call it a day. I've invited Rémy's parents and a few friends tonight for a small engagement celebration and I need to spend some time preparing."

***

Kate's idea of a small, impromptu celebration was in actuality a black-tie dinner and cocktail party. I begged Geneviève to drive me to my apartment so I could pick up a black dress and some high heels. I grabbed a suitable dress and shoes for Mina, as well, knowing she would want to look her best when she was formally introduced as Rémy's fiancée. They returned from Rouen with a gorgeous half-carat emerald cut diamond ring that Mina could not stop staring at. It was stunning, but too much for my taste. If I ever managed to wrangle an engagement ring out of Jack, I would prefer something smaller and more understated, which was a good thing considering Jack's income level versus Rémy's.

The party was a huge success, of course. Kate wouldn't throw a party that was anything less than perfect. Rémy's parents drove from Le Havre, where his father was a cardiologist and his mother was a pediatrician. Yeah, I know, right? I had met them a few times over the past year and got along with them really well. His father, Anton, had some mild psychic powers but had chosen to have little to do with the Conseil and his mother, Anaïs, was not a Seer. Because I hadn't met them before this last year, I had assumed Rémy and his parents were not close, but this was far from the truth. They had a wonderful relationship and made every effort to spend time together often, but hadn't had much of a chance since Rémy had moved to Rouen to attend university and then to America. We had spent quite a few weekends with them over the last year.

Phillipe made the official announcement after dinner and Rémy and Mina spent hours accepting congratulations and well wishes for their future. I spent most of the time talking with Geneviève and Arnaud and actually slipped out for a while to talk with Jack via Skype. He wanted to hear all the details of Mina's rescue again and especially wanted to hear the plans for my return to Albuquerque. I told him about our plan to stage an ascension and how I hoped to be free to go home soon afterward. He was dubious about the plan, but said he could support it if it meant I could finally come home. I assured him my main goal was to get home as soon as possible.

"That's good, querida, because I'm going crazy here. How long?"

I bit my lip. "I don't know for sure, Jack. I'm sorry. Maybe this weekend, I hope."

"Ally, I swear to God I'm gonna get on a plane and come over there if you're not home this weekend."

"Okay. This weekend for sure. I'll just come home," I promised. "I want to be there, Jack. You know that, don't you?" Did he think I *wanted* to stay away?

"Jesus, Ally, I know. I know, sweetheart. This separation is making me nuts. I need to be with you. We need to be together."

"I know," I whispered. "I hate this." I sniffed and

wiped my eyes. "Okay, enough of this! I don't want every time I talk to you to be such a drama scene. Tell me something good that's happened to you," I ordered.

He smiled slowly. "Yeah, okay. Let's see, I found out I got an A on my senior design project."

"Jack, that's great! Of course you got an A because you are brilliant! I'm so proud of you."

"Thanks, babe. Your turn."

"Geneviève had an ultrasound today and everything looks good so far with the baby," I said.

"That's great. Hey, Megan and I stopped by your mom's house yesterday and got to see Elijah. That brother of yours has gotten so big!"

"Oh, I miss him so much! He's probably forgotten all about me."

"No, he hasn't. He asked about his Awwy first thing." Elijah couldn't say my name correctly yet.

"Thanks, Jack. Have I mentioned lately that I am completely and totally in love with you?"

"It might have slipped your mind." He grinned. "Have I mentioned that I am crazy in love with you? I'd love to show you exactly how much."

"Ooh, that sounds promising. I really need to hurry home."

"Definitely."

***

We were up disgustingly early the next morning to make the final preparations for the fake ascension. The Conseil was meeting before lunch to discuss what action, if any, to take as a result of

Mina's kidnapping. I didn't really expect them to do anything useful, since they hadn't up to this point. The fact that it had taken them two days to even decide to meet was extremely frustrating, and I knew Rémy and Mina felt the same way. If they had stepped up and done something about Luc a long time ago, Michael might still be alive and I would be home in Albuquerque with the man I love.

We sat in Kate's private sitting room, sipping coffee sleepily and listening to Phillipe as he detailed how the ascension would go down. I drank herbal tea because my stomach was already upset as I worried about my horrible acting skills, upon which so much of this scheme rested. The others told me not to worry, that all I had to do was follow the plan and remember the prophecy Phillipe had created.

"I know, I know!" I snapped at Rémy when he told me for the fifth time not to create the blue glow too soon.

"Hey." Mina put her arms around me and rubbed my back. "You'll be fine. Stop worrying about it all. Everything will work perfectly and you'll be on your way home within a few days."

"Okay. Thanks, Mina." She always knew how to calm me down.

"Mina is correct," announced Kate. "Everything will be fine. All will go exactly as planned. Trust me. I'm psychic, after all." We all laughed half-heartedly and left to make our final preparations.

I sat in my room, staring into the mirror above my dressing table and wondering how I had arrived at this point in my life. It seemed like just yesterday

I was a normal high school student, worried about nothing more than homework and crushing on the cute guy who sat behind me in English. Now that cute guy was thousands of miles away and I was getting ready to fake a psychic ascension.

"Can I come in?" Mina peeked around my door.

"Sure."

She pulled a low stool close. "Are you doing okay, Ally?"

"Yeah." I sighed. "I guess. Are you and Rémy worried I'll chicken out?"

"No, of course not! We know you'll go through with it. You want this to be over just as much as we do. Maybe more. I know how badly you want to get home to Jack."

"I need him, Mina. I don't know how much longer I can do this alone." I sniffed and reached for a tissue.

"I know, I know." She took my hands and rubbed them. "We're going to make it through this, you know."

"I hope so, Mina. I really do." I wiped my eyes and squared my shoulders. "Okay, enough of that. I haven't had a chance to talk to you since we found you. How are you doing? Any nightmares or anything? God, Mina, you went through hell!"

"I'm fine. No nightmares. Having Rémy there to hold me helps. I mean, um, well…" she trailed off, blushing at what she had implied.

I laughed delightedly. "Oh, Mina! You should see how red your face is! Hey, it's great. I'm so glad you two finally worked everything out. You're happy, aren't you?"

She nodded. "So happy. I've loved him for so long. But you knew that, of course."

"I didn't need psychic powers to see that, sweetie. Or to see that it was reciprocated."

"Hey, your turn is just around the corner. It has to be."

"I hope so."

Rémy rapped lightly on the half-open door, interrupting us. "Mina, *mon coeur*, are you in there?"

I smiled at the love in his voice. "Come in, Rémy. She's here."

"Sorry about earlier, cherié." He apologized. "You'll do fine." He pulled Mina up and into his arms. "Are you ready for this, love?" He prevented her from answering by kissing her intensely.

"Jeez, you two. Get a room. And not mine." I pushed my way around them, heading to the closet for a scarf.

"If you're finished sitting here and freaking out, Ally, we can get this over with," he said wryly.

I rolled my eyes and led the way to the living room.

***

"I have asked Ally, Rémy, and Mina to join the Conseil today," Kate intoned a half-hour later as we all gathered. "We have all heard what happened to young Mina, but we will have an opportunity to hear the story in full and ask any clarifying questions." We spent nearly an hour re-telling the harrowing experience of Mina's kidnapping and answering questions from the Conseil members. I tried to contain my nervousness as I waited for the signal from Phillipe. It finally came as Hélène was asking for a clarification about how we knew where to find Mina.

"Ally, my dear, what is wrong?" he asked. This was it: the signal. Showtime.

"Um, I don't know. I feel funny. My hands are tingling." I held them up in front of my face. Out of the corner of my eye I saw Fionnuala blanch. I stood and walked to the center of the room.

Rémy came to my side, concerned. "Maybe you should sit down, cherié. You look pale." He put an arm around me as I began to sag weakly. Mina came to support my other side. The moment she touched me, connecting the three of us, I let the glow I had been practicing loose, enfolding the three of us in a soft blue light. I stood up straight, suddenly energized, and threw my head back. Now for the prophecy I tried desperately to remember.

"Behold the three, ascended. Alethiea, Oracle and speaker of truth and wisdom; Jessamine, heart of the Oracle and speaker of love and compassion; Rémy, guardian of both. The new day has dawned."

As soon as I finished, I let the blue glow die and the three of us collapsed on the floor. Quite the drama scene, I know. Hopefully it would be enough to convince the Conseil that I was the new Oracle. Kate had insisted we tell no one, not even Geneviève and Arnaud, that it was all fake. I was feeling plenty guilty about keeping the secret from them, especially, and hoped they would understand and forgive.

The ensuing fuss was everything we could have hoped for. We were "revived" and helped to the couch and given tea laced with brandy, which was gross. I spit most of mine back in my cup surreptitiously. I saw Rémy smirk, so maybe I wasn't as sneaky as I hoped. Of course, like any good Oracle, I didn't know what I had said during my trance so Phillipe told us. We were sent to rest in our rooms while the Conseil discussed what it meant. I waited five minutes before sneaking into Rémy's room, where he and Mina were waiting.

"Excellent work, Ally. It went exactly as planned," he said.

"What now?"

"We wait."

Great. I hate waiting.

Chapter Four

"Love, you mock us for your sport."
—Sophocles, *Antigone*

Kate finally called us to her sitting room. "Well, the good news is the Conseil absolutely believes the three of you have ascended. You gave a wonderful performance. It is only a matter of time before Luc hears about it."

"What's the bad news, Grandmére?" Rémy asked.

"They assume that Ally will remain here to take up the mantle of authority for the Conseil. Except Fionnuala and Caoimhe, of course, who are insisting you return to Ireland with them."

"Well, that's not going to happen," I said, trying to remain calm. "I'm going home. Tomorrow."

"I know, Ally dear. I fully support you. I'm finished trying to orchestrate your life. The rest of the Conseil will need to learn that the new Oracle sets her own agenda and decides where she will live. They are being difficult, however. I suggest you simply leave. Today, if possible."

I smiled and hugged her. "Thank you, Kate. Thanks for understanding."

"I will make the travel arrangements," Rémy offered. "We can leave within the hour. Mina and I will drive you to Paris."

I stopped by Geneviève and Arnaud's room before I left. I couldn't leave without saying goodbye to them. I hugged her and told her to keep in touch so I could hear about the baby.

"Of course, Ally. Oh, I'm going to miss you so much! I know you need to go home to be with your Jack, but I wish you could be two places at once."

I smiled and hugged her again. I knew they would be sympathetic to my need to return to New Mexico; neither of them shared the older Conseil members' feelings about the direction they wanted to see the Seer world take.

We were on the road to Paris within the hour. No one saw us leave since we simply left through the kitchen door and walked around to the garage, where André had stashed our suitcases in Rémy's car. Rémy said they would see me on my way back to the U.S. then return to Rouen to pack up Mina's and my apartment. I wondered what all this would do to their wedding plans.

"Don't worry about us, cherié," Rémy assured me. He brought Mina's hand up to his lips and they exchanged a look that made me smile. "We've got it figured out."

"I really want to be there, you idiot! Can you at least give me a hint as to when? I won't tell Kate, I promise." I figured they were trying to keep it from becoming the horrific spectacle that his grandmother was planning.

"I promise to tell you in time for you to be there," he assured me. "We want you there, of course. Well, at least Mina does."

I stuck my tongue out at him in the rearview mirror, but he just chuckled and kissed Mina's hand again.

We checked into Le Méridien Etoile, the hotel we always stayed in when we visited Paris. We usually shared a large suite, but this time Rémy handed me a key card to my own private suite and he and Mina disappeared into their own suite across the hall. We arranged to meet for dinner in a few hours and I spent the blessed alone time napping and showering. Three hours later and much refreshed, I met them downstairs in the lobby and we walked a couple blocks to Ballon et Coquillages, a tiny corner restaurant where Rémy had reserved a table. While they slurped down fresh oysters—as if those two needed an aphrodisiac—and some truly revolting-looking escargot, I had a salad and some really lovely cheese. Nobody does cheese like the French and I knew I would miss it when I left.

"So, I have you booked on an afternoon flight the day after tomorrow, cherié," Rémy said casually as we sipped white wine while waiting for our entrées.

"The day after tomorrow?" I exclaimed. "No, I want to go home tomorrow. Can you get it changed please, Rémy?"

"I tried, but all the flights were booked tomorrow. One day won't make such a difference."

"Besides," Mina cut in. "I really want you to go shopping with me tomorrow to look for a wedding dress. Please, Ally?" she begged.

"Fine." I sighed. "I guess I can wait one more day."

"Thanks, Ally. We'll make a day of it. Our last day in Paris. I'll even make us a spa reservation for the afternoon. You can go home to Jack extra beautiful."

"Okay, yeah. That sounds great." It would actually be nice to go home glowing and smooth. My nails were looking pretty ragged and my feet desperately needed attention.

Mina and I set off early the next morning, stopping for croissants and coffee before hitting the dress shops.

"Is he letting you get *any* sleep?" I asked wryly as she covered yet another yawn.

"Maybe I'm the one keeping him up," she countered with a sly grin. He had seen us off in the hotel lobby, handing Mina a credit card after he kissed her goodbye. He offered nothing about his own plans other than he had errands to run and waved us on our way.

Mina didn't want to look in bridal shops, which confirmed my belief that they had other plans up their sleeves about their wedding, but instead led the way to a few upscale boutiques, where she insisted we both try on dresses. At the last shop I fell in love with a summery, flowing dress in a light aqua I would have loved to wear on a special date with Jack, but it was way, way out of my price range so I firmly put it back on the rack and amused myself with the scarf rack while Mina bought an amazing ivory dress that she found. We stepped outside and she handed me a bag. Inside was the aqua dress, of course.

"No way, Mina. This dress cost a fortune! I can't let you buy this for me." I prepared to turn back to the shop to return it.

She grabbed my arm to stop me. "Rémy bought it for you and he can well afford it. Please, Ally. Let us do this for you."

"But I don't need it! You guys should save your money for the wedding."

"Pfft! I don't think you realize how wealthy he actually is. Besides, I like spoiling you. You look amazing in that dress. Jack will flip."

Playing to my vanity worked, and I graciously accepted the extravagant gift. We had lunch in a small bistro on the way to the spa, where we spent the afternoon—again courtesy of Rémy's credit card—getting buffed, polished, painted, and waxed. Mina talked me into a Brazilian wax, saying I might have reason very soon to be glad I had. Since I was certainly hoping the same thing as soon as I got home in a few days, I went along with her suggestion. I expected it to be painful and embarrassing, but the cosmetologist was so matter-of-fact and professional that it didn't bother me too much at all. It was lovely to walk out feeling fresh, smooth, and shiny *everywhere* and I had a feeling I had just developed an expensive addiction. We were due to meet Rémy back at the hotel lobby soon, so we caught a taxi just outside the spa. We walked through the revolving doors and I caught sight of

Rémy talking to a man whose back was to us. My heart began beating hard because it looked so much like—but it couldn't be, of course. Rémy noticed us and gestured for the man to turn around.

"Jack?" I whispered, disbelieving. I didn't know how or why, but it *was* him, here in Paris, grinning and walking toward me. I shoved my bags blindly at Mina and rushed into his outstretched arms, where I was crushed against his wonderfully hard chest. "Oh, my God. You're here! How—" My words were silenced as his mouth crashed down on mine. The entire lobby faded away as I melted against him, tasting, touching, and breathing him in for the first time in nearly a year.

"Surprise," he said against my lips a few moments later.

"It certainly is." I laughed. "Why? How?"

"I told you I was going to come get you," he said and kissed me again. Talking was overrated and could definitely wait. "Jack," I said when we finally came up for air. "I'm flying home tomorrow."

"No, you're not," Rémy interrupted. "I lied. You and Jack have tickets to return to the U.S. in three days. I'm sure you can find some way to amuse yourselves in the meantime."

I let go of Jack and hugged Rémy. "You did this. Thank you. I can't tell you how happy I am."

"I know, cherié." He hugged me close and whispered into my ear, "I didn't reserve a separate room for him, but I will if you like."

"That won't be necessary," I whispered back.

***

"Mina and I are going out for dinner," Rémy stated as Jack and I stared into each other's eyes. "I don't suppose you want to join us?"

"Nope," I said, grinning. "You guys go on without us. We'll catch up with you tomorrow." I broke eye contact finally and turned to hug Mina and retrieve the bags I had shoved at her earlier. "Thanks for everything today."

"Of course. Have fun tonight." She gave me a knowing look.

I smiled at her and turned back to Jack. "Let's go." I led him toward the elevators and punched the call button. "Where's your bag?"

"In your room. I got here a few hours ago and Rémy gave me a key card. I got a shower and shaved."

"Mmm. That's why you smell so good," I mumbled against his neck as I pulled him down for another kiss. We were interrupted by the arrival of the elevator and broke apart as a couple exited, smiling at us.

"Is that okay, Ally?" He pulled me into his arms once we were alone in the elevator. "I didn't mean to invade your room without asking. I can get my own room, if you want."

"Is that what you want?" I looked up into his dark eyes to try and gauge what he was feeling. This was where we would decide if the fact that we had been apart for a whole year was going to make things awkward or not. Would we be able to pick up where we left off and move forward? "Do you want to get your own room?"

"No."

I smiled. "Good." We needed to kiss again. "God, Jack. I'm so glad you're here."

"Me, too. I couldn't go one more day without you, querida." The elevator finally arrived at the 22nd floor and I led him to my suite. I fished the key card out of my bag and was about to swipe it, but he grabbed my hand gently. "Are you sure, Ally?"

I knew what he was asking, how important my answer was. I reached up, put my hands on either side of his face, forcing him to look at me. "I am absolutely, positively sure. I love you. It's our time, Jack, finally."

"Okay, then." He took the key card from my hand, swiped it in the lock, and led us into the suite. He didn't stop, but led me straight to the bedroom.

My heart was pounding, a mix of nerves and excitement. This was it. We were finally going to take the next step in our relationship. We were finally going to make love. We had waited so long. I saw his suitcase open on the floor, and smelled the lingering scent of his aftershave wafting from the bathroom. It was perfect.

He led me to the center of the room, took both my hands in his, and took a deep breath. "Ally Moran, I have loved you since you were 16 years old. I want to spend the rest of my life with you." He reached into his jeans pocket and pulled out a small velvet box, knelt down, and opened it to reveal a beautiful sapphire and diamond ring. "Will you marry me, Ally? I promise to spend the rest of my life trying to make you happy." He looked intense, adorably unsure, and unbearably handsome.

"You already make me so incredibly happy. And yes, I will marry you. Of course I will marry you." I couldn't keep the tears from spilling out onto my cheeks. I had long known he would never take this step without being engaged to me first. He grinned, took the ring out of the box, and placed it on my finger. It fit perfectly. "I love it, Jack."

He stood up and pulled me to him for a soul-wrenching kiss that I felt all the way to the tips of my toes. "Good. Tara helped me pick it out. She said you love sapphires, but if you want a bigger diamond—"

"Shh. It's perfect." I silenced him with another kiss. We kissed for several more minutes and the tenor of the kiss started to change from joy and happiness to intense desire. At least it did for me; Jack didn't try to push it any farther and his hands stayed firmly on my waist. I started to wonder when he was going step it up and take it to the next level. I finally pulled away and looked into his eyes, but he wouldn't quite meet mine. "Jack, what's wrong? Don't you want—" It finally occurred to me what was going on. "Are you scared?" I asked quietly.

He breathed out a huge breath. "Terrified," he admitted.

I smiled a little. He was the one with the experience, yet I was clearly going to have to take the lead if this was ever going to go anywhere. I don't know why I was so calm and collected suddenly, but I knew exactly what I wanted and I was more than ready for it. I stepped back slightly, reached down to the hem of my shirt, pulled it over my head, and dropped it on the floor. I was extremely glad I had decided to wear my pink lace bra that morning. Then I reached for his warm hand and placed it over my breast, smiling up into his handsome face. "It's me, Jack. Don't be scared of this. It's finally the right time for us."

That broke through his nervousness and he took over, scooping me into his arms and laying me gently on the bed, following me down.

***

I woke in the pre-dawn, encompassed in warmth and momentarily confused about where I was. Then I noticed the brown arm draped heavily across my chest and smiled, remembering the night before. I caught sight of the ring sparkling on my finger and smiled even wider. A glance at the bedside clock told me it was not yet six a.m. and I could feel Jack's deep breathing telling me he was still asleep. I carefully turned around so I could see my fiancé and watch him while he slept. He had let his hair grow out some over the past year and it was falling into his eyes. I let my eyes rove lovingly over his unshaven face down to his muscular chest. He had obviously spent a lot of time working out while we were apart; his arms and chest were bulging with muscle and his abs were rock hard and sexily defined. I felt my face go hot as I remembered that I now had intimate knowledge of what lie hidden beneath the blanket. He had gently and lovingly initiated me into the wonders of lovemaking and I had loved every minute of it. I'd had small glimpses over the past few years of the passion he kept tightly reined in, but it was nothing compared to what I had experienced last night. I had thought I knew every facet of him, but I was wrong. He showed me a whole new, unrestrained side of himself last night. I grinned as the memories of our lovemaking flashed in my mind. I wrenched my eyes back to his and saw that he was waking. He rubbed a hand over his face and opened his eyes.

"Morning," he said sleepily. "Have you been awake long?"

"No, just a few minutes."

"Were you staring at me while I slept, querida?" he asked with a chuckle.

"Just a little. I've missed looking at you. I can't seem to get my fill."

He reached to push my hair behind my ear. "Yeah, I know what you mean." He leaned in to kiss me softly. "Are you okay? I'm so sorry I hurt you last night."

"Oh, Jack, I'm absolutely fine. Please don't worry. It's perfectly normal, you know. I had to lose my virginity some time."

"I know, but I hate that you had to feel pain while I…"

"While you what? Tell me more. This sounds fascinating." I tried to sound serious.

He laughed softly and kissed me. "While I had the best night of my entire life. You were amazing."

"Really? What a coincidence, Mr. Ruiz. You were pretty amazing yourself. It was the best night of my entire life, as well," I teased and kissed him. "I'm so glad Mina insisted on that spa day yesterday."

"Yeah, well, I'm a huge fan." He had certainly been a very thorough fan. "Remind me to thank her later." He kissed me deeply and then pushed himself up on his elbow to lean over me. "Are you sure you're okay?"

"Better than okay. I'm amazing, remember?" We both laughed as he kissed me again. "Yes, I'm fine, I promise." I was slightly sore, but in the most delicious way possible and didn't regret it in the slightest.

He pulled away slightly and smiled at me. "Marry me, Ally."

I reached up and stroked his face. "You already asked me that last night." I showed him the ring. "Remember? I said yes, by the way."

He took my hand and kissed my fingers just below the engagement ring then entwined his hand with mine and set them on the pillow above my head. "I do remember. Marry me today."

"What? What are you talking about?"

He leaned in to kiss me. "Marry me today, here in Paris." He looked intently into my face, all trace of teasing gone.

"You're serious." I sat up, pulling him with me. "Talk to me."

"I don't want to wait, Ally. We've seriously spent enough time waiting. Rémy and Mina are getting married before a justice of the peace later today and he's arranged for us to be married, as well, but only if you're okay with it."

I knew that getting married in France involved a legal ceremony in front of a judge before any optional religious ceremony, and there was a strict residency requirement for at least one half of the couple. "I thought there was a waiting period, like two weeks or something."

"I'm pretty sure Rémy can bribe his way out of anything. It's all arranged, querida, but only if you're okay with it."

"Oh my God. Wow. We could actually get married today? What about our families, Jack? Won't they be disappointed not to be there?" I desperately wanted to marry him, but could I do it without anyone knowing?

"I've been talking to Rémy about this for several days and I warned everyone back home before I left. It would be similar to what Rémy and Mina are doing: we'd have a civil ceremony here and then repeat our vows in front of a priest back home. Trina's already planning a big reception. But only if you're comfortable with it."

"You talked to Grams and my mom?"

"I even called your dad," he explained. "He gave his blessing." At my incredulous look, he continued. "Well, he gave his blessing contingent upon getting to walk you down the aisle as soon as we get back to Albuquerque. I'm pretty sure they all realized it was inevitable, so they gave in fairly graciously." He again pushed my hair behind my ears and framed my face with his hands. "I really hope you'll say yes, Ally. I don't want to wait. We have waited and been separated long enough. I want it to be you and me from here on out. I want to live with you, sleep with you, eat with you—"

I gasped. "Jack, what about Tara? Where is she going to live when you move in?" She had been living in my house by herself for the last year, taking care of Wicky and the yard. "I don't think she's going to want to move back with her parents. And I don't really want her living with us."

He grinned, obviously sensing victory. "I don't think you need to worry about her, babe. She's already moving her stuff to the apartment with Mat. He actually hasn't spent a night at home in the last six months or so."

"What? Mat's been shacking up with Tara in my house?" I squeaked. "God, I hope not in my bed!"

He laughed and pulled me down to lie in his arms. "I don't think so. We can change the sheets when we get back, just in case. I helped him buy a ring before I left," he confessed.

"Oh my God!" I exclaimed again.

"Hey, could you act surprised when she shows you the ring? I don't think I was supposed to tell you. I'm unable to keep a secret from you."

"That's a good thing. So, what time is our wedding?" I asked. Of course I would marry him today. I got the best of both worlds: an intimate, private ceremony with the man I loved and a family wedding back home.

He leaned over me again. "Seriously, Ally?" I nodded. He leaned down to kiss me thoroughly. "You have just made me the happiest man in Paris."

I rolled over to lie on top of him. "Really? I was kind of thinking I could make you even happier, if we have time."

He looked at the clock. "We definitely have time."

Chapter Five

"I go to wed the lord of the dark waters."
—Sophocles, *Antigone*

Three hours later, after more lovemaking and a shared shower—delightful, but rather more time-consuming than a lone shower—we were nearly ready to meet Rémy and Mina for a late breakfast before our joint marriage ceremonies.

"We can have a big wedding back home if you want, querida," he said as he helped me zip the gorgeous aqua dress Mina had bought for me the day before. "You can have a real wedding dress. I really like this one, however." He pushed the spaghetti strap down and kissed my bare shoulder.

I leaned my head back against him and let out a moan as his warm lips traversed my skin. "If you keep that up, we'll miss our wedding." I saw him grin salaciously in the mirror. "And I don't want a big wedding. I was thinking we could have a small ceremony, with just our families in Trina's backyard. I'll wear this dress. Unless you want a big wedding?" I asked as I turned in his arms.

"Sweetheart, with my family it will be a big wedding." We both smiled, realizing his vast number of relatives would indeed turn any ceremony into a big event. "But a backyard ceremony sounds great. I love this dress." He leaned down to taste my other shoulder.

"Mmmm," I pulled his head up and kissed him lingeringly. "We better go. I can hear your stomach growling. I feel bad for keeping you prisoner all night and not feeding you any dinner."

"You can keep me prisoner any time you want. Dinner was the last thing on my mind last night."

I laughed with him. "Yeah, mine too. But we need to keep up our strength, you know."

Rémy and Mina were already seated in the breakfast room downstairs when Jack and I arrived. "You really need to stop smirking, Rémy," I said as I reached for the coffee pot.

He laughed as Mina elbowed him. "I can't help it, cherié. You are blushing furiously and Jack is looking disgustingly smug. I trust all went well?"

"None of your business. So, I understand we're all getting married this morning?" I asked nonchalantly. At Mina's delighted look I thrust my left hand with its new ring at her.

"Oh, Ally! It's gorgeous. I'm so happy for you. This is going to be wonderful! We'll share an anniversary!"

"So, how do you think Kate and Phillipe will react to you two getting married secretly?" I asked as I bit into a croissant.

"It's not a secret," Rémy said. "I called them

yesterday. This is how it's done in France. We are required by law to have a *mariage civil* in front of a government official before any other type of ceremony. The only secret is that Jack is here and you two are also getting married. It truly is best for you to present both the Conseil and the Council with a *fait accompli* in this regard. I have the distinct feeling they have plans for you, as their new Oracle, that don't include returning to the United States with an American boyfriend."

"Well, in a few hours she'll be my wife and then no one can separate us." Jack took my hand and kissed the palm. I leaned over and kissed him on the mouth, not caring that we were in the middle of a restaurant.

"Don't mind us," Rémy said with a chuckle.

We took a taxi to the city hall, where our ceremonies would take place. I knew Rémy must have called in quite a few favors and spent thousands of euros to bypass all the legal requirements to make this possible.

"Thank you, Rémy, for doing this. You don't know what it means to us." I leaned against him and squeezed his arm.

"It is my pleasure, cherié. It is long past time we three forged our own path and stop letting Luc and the other Seers make all the decisions. Now, I'm sorry to say that the upcoming ceremony is not very romantic, but it is perfectly legal. You will be married, at least. You can exchange rings and vows when you get home in front of a priest, if you wish."

"I think Trina is already planning something for

us," I said. "What about you? Will you have another ceremony or anything?"

"Oui. Grandmére has a reception planned for early next week."

"At least this gives me time to find you a ring, Jack," I said.

"Maybe we can find one here in Paris. I have yours that matches the engagement ring and I'd feel more married if we had wedding rings. I'm not going to understand much of the ceremony, so I'll need you to tell me when to say 'I do.'"

"You actually don't even say that," Rémy said. "You'll just say 'oui' when the time comes. That means 'yes.'"

"Yeah, I know that." Jack rolled his eyes.

"Let's hear it, then," Rémy taunted.

"Wee," Jack gritted out. Rémy cringed and Jack started muttering Spanish curse words.

"Boys!" I exclaimed as Mina elbowed Rémy in the ribs. "I definitely like the idea of exchanging rings here," I soothed Jack. "And don't worry. I'll translate the ceremony for you."

The taxi dropped us in front of the city hall for the 17th arrondissement and we went inside. We had to wait for about thirty minutes before the adjunct was available and then were ushered into an office. Rémy and Mina went first and then it was our turn. We stood face to face in front of a table and I translated the words of the official for Jack. We said 'oui' at the proper time, kissed, and within about five minutes were pronounced husband and wife. We signed the *livret de famille* and were on our way.

Outside, on the steps of the city hall, Jack pulled me into his arms for a better kiss. "I love you, Mrs. Ruiz."

I beamed up at him. "And I love you, Mr. Ruiz." We pulled apart to see Rémy and Mina still kissing passionately. "Hey, Monsieur and Madame Giles! Don't we have reservations for lunch soon?" They broke apart, grinning like the love-struck idiots we all were, and led us down the street toward the restaurant where Rémy had reserved a private room. We had a lovely champagne luncheon with many toasts and I ended up rather tipsy, which seemed to amuse Jack.

"Well, this has been fun, but I think I need to get my bride back to the hotel. She probably needs a nap to sleep off all this champagne."

I plopped down on his lap and proceeded to kiss his neck. "I love your neck, Jack. You smell so good. You always smell so good." I ended on a hiccough, which made everyone laugh, including me. I couldn't stop once I started, however. Everything was so funny.

"Well," Jack said with a laugh. "We need to go." He stood, setting me on my feet, where I wobbled on my high heels. "Come on, babe. Let's get you back for a nap."

"Well, *someone* kept me up all night," I said with a yawn.

"Jack, you'd better get her back before she tells us more than we really need to know," Mina advised.

He held me close to his side and led me outside to catch a taxi back to our hotel. I vaguely remembered Rémy saying that he and Mina would stay to settle the bill and see us later. I dozed against Jack in the cab and reluctantly roused when we reached the hotel. He paid the driver and gave him a decent tip along with a credible 'merci.'

"Hmm, that sounded great, Jack. You're learning quickly." I hiccoughed again.

"Yeah, I'm a real linguist. Let's get you upstairs, babe. You're nearly asleep on your feet."

"I'm sorry. I should be more fun on our wedding night."

He punched the button for the elevator. "Oh, I'm not worried, querida. We've got hours until it's our wedding night. We can have a nice long nap on our wedding afternoon. *Someone* didn't let me get much sleep last night, either."

"I wonder who that could be?" I asked as I nuzzled his neck in the elevator.

"You keep that up and there won't be a lot of napping, Mrs. Ruiz."

"Mmmm, I like the sound of that."

"Which? The no napping or the 'Mrs. Ruiz'?" he asked, laughing.

"Yes."

He swiped his key card at our door and then scooped me into his arms to carry me over the threshold. "It's tradition," he whispered against my lips.

Our room had been cleaned, our bed made, and there was a bottle of champagne in an ice bucket and a tray of chocolate-dipped strawberries on the bedside table, compliments of Rémy, of course. The last thing I needed was more champagne right now, but I was sure we would get around to it later.

I turned around and presented my back to my husband. "Unzip me?" He was quick to comply, kissing the skin he bared as he unzipped.

"You are so soft. I have dreamed of touching you like this for so long."

I turned in his arms, loosened his tie, and began unbuttoning his shirt. "Me too. No more cold showers for either of us." I stepped back and pushed the straps off my shoulders, letting the aqua dress pool at my feet.

We finally got around to napping an hour or so later; we opened the champagne several hours after that. We ordered dinner from room service even later.

"So, what do you want to see in Paris, Jack?" I asked in the wee hours of the night as I lay in his arms, swirling my fingers through his chest hair.

"I've already seen everything I came to see, querida. I plan to see it a lot more, though."

I laughed and sat up enough to kiss his jaw. "Well, we can't stay in bed for three whole days. You can't come all the way to Paris and not want to see any of it."

"I didn't come to sightsee, babe." He kissed the top of my head. "And I could easily stay in bed with you for at least a week." He pulled me on top of him and my hair formed a curtain around our heads. "But I need to remember that this is all new for you. I should probably think about letting you out of bed tomorrow, at least for a little while. Where should we go? You probably know all the really cool places."

"I'll get back to you on that," I said while kissing his neck and moving down to his chest. I had other things to think about right then.

***

We spent the morning strolling through the Tuileries Garden and along the Place de la Concorde. We snapped a few photos in front of the Louvre pyramid, but Jack had no desire to go inside, especially once he saw the hideous lines. We found him a simple platinum wedding band in a shop on the Rue de Rivoli and then I took him to my favorite bridge in Paris, the Pont de l'Archevêché, where we exchanged our rings, placing them on each other's fingers while we privately made our vows to each other.

"Aletheia Grace, from the moment you walked into my English class four years ago, I knew you were special. You sat right in front of me, torturing me, every day. I used to make excuses to lean forward on my desk just so I could smell your hair. Sometimes you would lean back and your gorgeous red ponytail would reach my desk. I would reach out and touch the end. That would make my day. I was never going to talk to you, until the day you almost passed out in class. I knew I wasn't good enough for someone like you, but you didn't care. You stuck to me like glue and didn't care about all the stupid, idiotic stuff I had done. You never saw the troublemaker I was; you saw the real me. The day you insisted on coming to my probation hearing was the day I knew I was head-over-heels in love with you. Now you're my wife and I can't believe how lucky I am. I promise to love you and respect you until my dying day, and then forever." He placed the matching diamond and sapphire band on my finger next to the engagement ring he had placed there two days ago.

I sniffed and wiped away the tears that streamed down my cheeks. "Jackson Iván, from the moment I walked into my English class and saw you sitting in the back of the room looking dark, mysterious, and gorgeous," I smiled into his eyes as he chuckled self-consciously, "I was drawn to you in a way I didn't begin to understand. I just had to sit as close to you as I could, and I *always* sit at the front of the classroom." We both laughed, as we knew it was true. "I thought my crush was hopeless, you know. Why would a guy like you want to be with a girl like me? But you did, Jack, and I'm so glad. You have loved me and protected me for four years and now, for some amazing reason, you have become my husband. I can't believe how lucky I am. I promise to love you and care for you today, tomorrow, and forever." I pushed the ring I had just bought onto his finger then stood on tip-toe to kiss him. We were lost to the world for a few blessed moments until the sound of applause broke through our love-soaked consciousness. A small crowd had gathered around us as we had our private ceremony and was now cheering us. We laughed and kissed again for their benefit and gratefully accepted their offers to snap our picture on the beautiful bridge overlooking the Seine.

We crossed the bridge and strolled through the

Île de la Cité, the island center of Paris in the middle of the Seine, and stopped to admire Notre Dame Cathedral before crossing to the Île Saint-Louis. We had lunch at a charming outdoor bistro and watched the other tourists go by, then I took him to Berthillon for the world's best sorbet. We spent a magical day strolling hand-in-hand through Paris neighborhoods until it was time to return to the hotel to change for dinner. We were meeting Rémy and Mina for a last meal before they returned to Rouen the following day. We would catch our flight back to Albuquerque the day after that and our magical honeymoon in Paris would be over.

In the midst of my extreme happiness I found myself sad to think about not seeing Rémy and Mina after tonight. "I'm going to miss you both so much!" I said.

"Jack is clearly not keeping you occupied enough if you already have time to think about missing us," Rémy teased.

"Shut up! He's keeping me plenty busy. And I've changed my mind: I'm not going to miss you at all. I will miss Mina, however." I stuck my tongue out at him.

"Well, you won't have to miss her for long because we'll be moving to Albuquerque in a month or two at the most," he said blithely as he sipped his wine.

"What? Oh my goodness, that's great! You guys are going to live in the States? I don't imagine the Conseil or your grandparents are going to be fans of that plan."

"Well, I was thinking our new Oracle could have

a well-timed prophecy that hints at the importance of the chosen three living in close proximity," he suggested.

"I think that could be arranged." I nodded. "As happy as I am to be married to this guy," I paused to kiss Jack's cheek, "and to be going home, I don't want to lose you and Mina. I guess I want it all."

"We think it's important to stay together, as well," explained Mina. "Rémy is going to concentrate on opening an American branch of the family business and I can do my website work anywhere. And I don't want to be so far away from my best friend, either. I guess I want it all too."

I had to hug her after that super-sweet statement and it turned into a bit of a tear-fest as we said goodbye for a few months. Hey, can you blame us? We had both been through quite the emotional gamut over the past week. Jack and Rémy let us have a moment before they pulled their teary wives away and took us back to the hotel.

***

"I'm scared, Jack." I lay in the warmth and comfort of my husband's arms, but reality was rearing its ugly head. "What if Luc follows us back to Albuquerque? What if he doesn't know that I've supposedly ascended or what if he doesn't care? Am I putting everyone in danger by going home?"

"I don't have the answers, querida. I just know that I love you and I need you with me. You're my wife and I'll do whatever it takes to keep you safe." He followed this with a fierce kiss.

"But who will keep you safe?" I whispered against his lips.

"Oh, I'm not too worried. You're pretty badass with that blue light thing. I think we'll be fine. It's time to live our lives, not borrow trouble. We're on our honeymoon, babe. I better think of something to get your mind off Luc. I'm clearly not doing my job if you've got time to think about him while we're in bed together." He was as good as his word and managed to keep me delightfully busy for the rest of the night.

I woke the next morning with the sun streaming in through an opening where the curtains didn't quite meet. I was alone in the king-sized bed, so I put on one of the plush hotel robes and went to the other room to look for my missing husband. I found him sitting in one of the side chairs, sipping coffee and reading the paper, wearing the glasses he sometimes wore to read. I tip-toed up behind him and put my arms around his neck.

"You managed to find a *New York Times*?"

"Yeah. I wanted to let you sleep in. I feel bad about how much I've been keeping you up."

"Mmm." I slipped my hand into the front of his robe as I nibbled his earlobe. "You feel *really* bad, don't you? Come back to bed, Jack," I whispered.

He grinned and set aside his paper and coffee and pulled me across his lap. "Have I told you how much I love being married to you, Mrs. Ruiz?" He untied the belt of my robe and pushed it off my shoulder.

"Not for at least two hours. You are seriously behind schedule." I reached up to remove his glasses and set them on the side table. "Will you come back to bed now?"

"We don't need a bed."

He was right.

***

We did finally leave the hotel room in time to see the Eiffel Tower light up at night and enjoy a final romantic dinner in Paris at a lovely restaurant overlooking the Seine. The next morning we caught a cab to Charles de Gaulle airport for our flight home. I sat next to Jack in first class, sipping orange juice drowsily—we had not spent a lot of time sleeping on our last night—and thinking about how good it would be to see my family again. I wouldn't trade the last three days for anything in the world, but it was time to go home.

"Jack, what about Soda?" I asked.

"You want a soda? Let me get the flight attendant." He started to reach for the call button.

"No." I grabbed his hand and kissed it. "I mean Sodapop, your dog."

He laughed and leaned in to kiss me. "What about him, querida?"

"Well, I know you haven't been able to keep him with you at the apartment and I know you miss him."

"Sure I do, but he keeps Megan company." I could hear the longing in his voice, for both his pet and his sister.

"How does he do with cats? Can he come live with us?"

"I don't know, babe. We can try. You sure you want my stinky dog in your pretty little house, though? He's a mess and he sheds like crazy."

"Hey." I put my hand on his face and forced him to look at me. "*Our* house, Jack. What's mine is yours, remember? It's part of that whole marriage thing we did a few days ago. And that means that stinky, hairy dog of yours is half mine. I just hope he doesn't eat Wicky."

"I'm pretty sure Wicky could take him. Do you have any idea how much I love you?" he asked.

"Maybe a little bit," I answered as he kissed me. "What about Megan?"

He sighed. "I don't know, Ally. I never meant for Trina and Manny to have to take care of her for so long. They raised their own kids already. They should have a break, but—"

"Why can't she live with us? We'll have plenty of room."

"I can't ask you to take on raising a child just because you married me. You're only twenty years old, not even finished with college. It would be too much," he said, but again I could hear the longing in his voice.

"And you're only 22 and just about to start graduate school. We can do it, Jack!" I urged. "She's your sister. She's my sister now too. I think she should live with us."

"You sure you know what you're getting into, querida? A nine-year-old could really cramp our style."

"We'll manage. Yes, I'm sure. I am the Oracle, remember?" I tried to look superior.

"Of course you are," he said, laughing. "Okay, we'll talk to Trina and Manny, but after the wedding, all right? And we need to ask Megan what she wants. She might not want to live with me."

"Of course she will. She practically worships you."

"Yeah, well, I'm sure she'll get over it, especially when she finds out she has to do chores at our house too." He put his arm around me and pulled my head down to his chest. "Get some sleep, Ally."

Tara and Mat were waiting for us at the Albuquerque Sunport when we finally arrived after a lengthy delay at Washington Dulles.

"Ooooh, my gosh!" my best friend squealed when she saw me. "Let me see the ring! I can't believe you went and got married without me! I'm so mad I wasn't there! You better let me be maid of honor at your fake ceremony this weekend!"

"Of course." I laughed and hugged her close. "And you're one to talk, you little slut! Shacking up with Mat in my house?"

She laughed. "Yeah, well I'm sure you guys waited until your wedding night, huh?" She let go and moved to hug Jack. "Big mouth! You just can't keep a secret, can you?"

"Not from Ally," he said as he laughed and hugged her.

"Come on, babe." Mat pulled her away. "These guys look exhausted. Let's get them home. We can get all caught up tomorrow. Jack, we got all your stuff moved to Ally's house and got Tara moved into the apartment."

"Let me see your ring!" I grabbed Tara's hand. "You better not have said no!"

"Seriously, Jack?" She punched him on the arm. "Stop telling her everything! I wanted to have one surprise!"

"Oh, Tara, it's gorgeous! When's the wedding?" I asked.

"In August. We're still trying to find the perfect venue for the reception." She put her arm through mine and chattered about the wedding plans all the way through the airport to the baggage claim.

"Man, you are so lucky!" I heard Mat tell Jack. "You didn't have to go through all this wedding crap."

"What's that, Mateo?" Tara rounded on them.

"Nothing, babe." He held his hands up in surrender. "I love you."

She narrowed her eyes at him then turned back around, picking up right where she left off.

I saw Mat mouth 'lucky' at Jack again before I turned back to Tara.

"So, how did you like Paris?" I heard Mat ask him.

"Is that where we were? Huh," Jack mused and then they both laughed.

Boys!

Part Two: Power

Chapter Six

"Go then if you must, but remember, no matter how foolish your deeds, those who love you will love you still."
—Sophocles, Antigone

"Are you sure about this, Ally? Because if you have even the slightest bit of doubt, you don't have to go through with it. I'll tell everyone; you won't have to say anything or see anyone," my dad offered hopefully.

I smiled at him sadly and kissed his cheek. "Thanks, Dad, but I'm sure. We're already married, you know. Even if I don't go through with this, we're still married."

"Well, it seems kind of fishy to me. I'm not sure it was legal. We could probably get it annulled or something," he grumbled.

"Oh, Dad." I hugged him fully. "I love Jack and I would still go through with this even if we weren't already married. Now come on and walk me down the aisle, okay? Don't forget you owe me a dance later at the reception."

"All right, sweetheart. If you're sure. He's a good man. I couldn't let you go otherwise." He sniffed and patted his pockets.

"Here." I handed him a tissue. "I love you, Dad. I'm so glad you're here."

"I love you too. Now, let's get you married. Again."

The ceremony was perfect, the day was perfect, and everything was perfect. I wore my beautiful aqua dress again and Jack wore a suit and tie. My dad walked me up the makeshift aisle in Manny and Trina's backyard toward my groom, who was waiting for me with a grin on his face. He held his hand out as we approached and I gladly clasped it and took my place by his side. Jack and I stood in front of Father Andrews, Jack's parish priest, and said the traditional wedding vows and exchanged the rings we had taken off an hour ago. We took communion and then shared a kiss before we were introduced as Mr. and Mrs. Jack Ruiz. It was beautiful and nice to be able to enjoy it without all the pre-wedding jitters most couples have to deal with. We had been able to sleep in before we had to be at the university for Jack's graduation ceremony midmorning, and then grabbed a quick lunch before heading over to Manny and Trina's. We had convinced Trina that one party would more than suffice for his graduation and our wedding. Tara and Megan were my attendants, while Mat and his brother, Paul, served as Jack's. We managed to get my little brother, Elijah, to toddle up the aisle with a ring bearer's pillow, but he took off in the wrong direction when he spotted my mother. Everyone laughed, which made Elijah cry, but Brian held him until he stopped.

The reception/graduation party was great and a wonderful way to catch up with family and friends that I hadn't seen in a year. Shelly was there with her son, Nathan, now five, and her baby girl, Emma, who was nearly two. There was a huge stack of gifts; some for Jack alone and some for the two of us, but we certainly hadn't registered anywhere. We would come to Trina's tomorrow for a brunch and gift-opening extravaganza. We both endured quite a bit of teasing about our upcoming wedding night number two, but it didn't bother us.

Manny pulled us aside later in the afternoon. "Listen, you two. I want to take your Aunt Trina away for a vacation next week. I've booked a cruise, but it's a surprise. She'll make up a hundred excuses if I tell her, so I'm just going to whisk her away next Friday. I know it's soon, but can you keep Megan while we're gone? I don't want to ask Marcos." He referred to Jack's father, who had shown up for the ceremony, but left soon after. He had made some progress toward being present in Megan's life, but nobody was ready for her to stay at Marcos' apartment.

"Of course, Manny," I assured him. "It's not too soon. We're happy to have her." I looked up at Jack and nodded in encouragement.

"Yeah, Manny. In fact, we were planning to talk to you about the possibility of Megan coming to live with us. Permanently," Jack said hesitantly.

Manny sighed and seemed to relax. "Well, I won't pretend I'm not glad to talk about it. We love Megan, but the fact is I'm getting ready to retire, at least semi-retire. Paul is taking over most of the operation of the shop, and I want to enjoy our golden years," he said as he chuckled a bit. "I don't feel old, so now's the time to enjoy the fruits of our labors. Trina and I worked hard for a lot of years and we deserve some time to ourselves, Jack. I'm still crazy in love with that woman and I want to spoil her some."

"Manny, I never meant for you and Trina to raise us," Jack said. I noticed his eyes were shining slightly. I put my arm around him.

"I know, Jackson, but shit happens, son." It lightened the mood and we all laughed. "We just have to pick up and carry on. Do the best we can. I'm very proud of you, Jack."

"Thank you, Manny." They hugged and thumped each other on the back.

"And I'm glad you came into Jack's life, young lady. You make him happy. That's all Trina and I could ever ask for." Now it was my turn to hug him tearfully. "Okay, enough of this sappy stuff." He sniffed and wiped his eyes. "I'll bring Megan over Thursday. That'll give you a few days by yourselves. Let's see how it goes while we're on this cruise, then we can talk about a more permanent arrangement. Let's see what Megan wants."

***

"Meg, do you want to go swimming today? Tara invited us." I knocked on Megan's half-closed bedroom door and peeked in to find my sister-in-law sitting at her desk, drawing.

"Sure." She didn't look up from her latest creation. "When?"

"After lunch." I crossed to her desk and peered over at shoulder at the very credible likeness of Sodapop and Wicky. She was using the new set of drawing pencils we bought her for her birthday. "That's wonderful, Meg! You are so talented. Who's this one for?" Our refrigerator was already plastered with her artwork.

She shrugged noncommittally. "Maybe Tara. I feel bad that she and Mat can't have a dog or a cat at their apartment."

I hid my smile. I knew that Tara wasn't pining for a pet of any kind. "That would be nice. You could give it to her this afternoon." Megan had been living with us for two months; she had come to stay while Manny and Trina were on their cruise and had never left. It seemed natural for her to be here. Trina had been reluctant at first, but had relented when she saw how happy Megan and Jack were to be together. She insisted on keeping Megan's room intact at their house so she would feel at home whenever she stayed there, which was at least every other weekend; Trina felt strongly that Jack and I needed some time alone. Megan was an exceptionally easy child; she was almost unnaturally quiet most of the time, preferring to spend time reading or drawing. She never fussed when it was time to do chores and nearly always picked up after herself. Jack was really the only person who could get her to be silly or talkative and it was good to see them together, playing a game or working on a project of some sort. It had been a smooth transition installing her in our home with one exception: she had frequent nightmares and ended up in bed with Jack and me four or five nights per week. She had done the same thing with Trina and Manny; Jack said she had been having them since she was two years old. The first night she had appeared at my bedside, bedraggled stuffed pig in hand and tears streaming down her little face, just about broke my heart. After double-checking that both Jack and I were wearing pajamas—hello, newly married—I scooted over to let her in our bed. She crawled over me to lie between us, smiling when Jack had sleepily told her we formed an impenetrable barrier against nightmares. I had expressed my concerns to Grams, but she assured me that Megan would almost certainly outgrow the nightmares within a few years. So we just concentrated on cuddling and soothing away the bad dreams for now. "I'm going to wash your sheets. Can I wash Mr. Gordo too?" I held up her stuffed pig that had seen better days. At her look of consternation I added, "I'll put him in a pillowcase, sweetie. He'll be fine, I promise. Think of how nice and fresh he'll smell."

She nodded reluctantly. We were very careful about Mr. Gordo because he was one of the last things her mother had given her before she died.

"Let me get this wash going and then I'll make us some sandwiches for lunch, okay?"

"I'll make lunch, Ally." She put a final touch on her drawing and then skipped into the kitchen to fix lunch while I stripped her bed. I noticed a few new drawings hanging on the wall as I pulled the sheets off. They were all different views of the same face: a boy about Megan's age. She had captured the sad expression in his eyes perfectly. I made a mental note to see about getting her some drawing lessons; this kind of talent should be fostered.

Over grilled cheese sandwiches we discussed our plans for the afternoon. "I thought we could invite Mat and Tara over for a barbecue this evening after we swim. We could pick up groceries on the way home. Would you like that?" She nodded, her mouth full of sandwich. "We have a fitting tomorrow for our bridesmaid dresses, you know. Maybe we could do some school shopping for you while we're out." She was going to start fifth grade in a few weeks and although she hadn't grown much over the summer, she could use some new clothes. "Do you want to invite a friend tonight?" I was worried she didn't seem to have a lot of friends her own age. She shrugged and shook her head. "What about Mikayla? We could call her, if you want."

"She's at camp."

"Oh." Why didn't I think of camp for Megan? I tried to think of anyone else we could invite and came up empty.

She cleared my empty plate and put it in the dishwasher. "It's okay, Ally. I don't need a friend tonight. I have you and Jack. Don't worry about me." Sometimes I wondered which one of us was the adult.

We spent the afternoon swimming with Tara; rather Megan and Tara swam. I mostly stayed in the shade and slathered on SPF 50 sunscreen: the curse of a redhead! Tara was all golden brown skin and blonde hair in her barely-there blue bikini while Megan was naturally brown, romping in her sparkly pink one-piece. Jack nixed the bikini she had chosen first, saying that no sister of his would wear so little in public. Strange that he loved it when I wore one.

"Good lord! Look at all these gorgeous girls at the pool today!" Mat leaned against the pool fence and wolf whistled, his paramedic shirt open and untucked in the New Mexico summer heat. *"¡Qué bonita!"*

Tara sashayed over to give him a kiss across the fence. "Get changed and join us," she suggested.

Once he got in the pool, the afternoon swim became much more boisterous as he chased Tara and Megan around the pool. Tara let herself be caught frequently; I threw a beach ball at them once when they skirted a bit too close to an R-rating for the afternoon.

"Sorry, Ally! I can't help myself around this sexy lady." He picked her up and threw her, causing a huge splash that soaked me in my lawn chair.

I was wet anyway, so I jumped in for a few minutes more and we played Marco Polo until I decided it was time to head home. "Come on, Meg. We still need to stop by the grocery store and your brother will be home soon."

Tara and Mat waved us away at their apartment

door and judging by where his hands were headed, they'd probably be late for the barbecue.

***

I stepped out of the shower later that evening, wrapped myself in a fluffy towel, and grabbed my lotion.

"I would be happy to do that for you, querida," Jack reached over my head and took the bottle out of my hand.

"Oh, you would, huh? You, sir, are helpful," I teased.

"Yep, that's me." He plopped me on the edge of the bathroom counter and proceeded to pour lotion into his hands, warming it between his palms before smoothing it on my leg. "I always try to be helpful, ma'am."

"Is Megan asleep?"

"Yeah, she crashed right away. You must have worn her out swimming this afternoon. We have at least a little while until she joins us. I plan to take full advantage of it. And you." He let his hand sneak under the edge of the towel.

"Ooh, I like the sound of that." I leaned over to kiss his dark head as he knelt in front of me. "I'm worried about her, Jack."

"You don't think we should let her sleep with us?"

"No, it's not that. Grams said she'll grow out of that soon. No, I'm worried that she doesn't really have any friends and she doesn't seem to mind."

"Hmm. Well, school starts soon. Maybe she'll

find some new friends in her class. She's so quiet. And serious." He moved to smoothing lotion on my arms, which was playing havoc with my ability to concentrate. "We've got a lot on our plates with Tara and Mat's wedding coming up, babe. Why don't we table this particular worry for a few weeks?" He started at my fingertips and kissed his way up. "We'll figure it out later. Right now we have that whole bed in there to ourselves for a few hours. It has been at least ten hours since I have held you in my arms, and that, my dear wife, is way too long." He dispensed with the towel and carried me to bed.

**

I ran. Tripped and fell, cutting my hands and knees on broken glass. Cried out. I picked myself up and ran again. Searching, crying out. For what? Who? Someone was missing and my heart was breaking. My hands were shaking with cold and fear. Where was—what? What was I looking for? I screamed in frustration.

"What?" Jack jerked awake.

I must have screamed in my sleep for real. I woke sitting up in bed, tears streaming down my face.

"Ally, what's wrong?" He put his arms around my waist and pulled me close. "God, you're shaking, sweetheart. Did you have a nightmare?"

I shook my head. "Vision," I managed to choke out. I knew enough by now to be able to tell the difference between an ordinary nightmare and a vision.

"Okay, okay," he smoothed my hair out of my face. "It's all right, babe. I'm here. I've got you." He rocked me in his arms. I clung to him and tried to get my breathing back under control.

"Jack?" Megan's small voice was laced with fear as she peeked around the doorway. "Is Ally okay?"

"Oh, yeah, squirt. Ally's fine. She just had a real bad dream."

I hated that I had scared her. I reluctantly pulled myself away from Jack, sniffed, and held my arms out to her. "Come here, Meg. I'm fine." She climbed on the bed, relieved, as my cell phone rang on the bedside table. "It's Rémy. Can you get it Jack?"

"Sure," he muttered as he got up and hurried around the bed to answer the phone. I heard him whisper 'shit' as he stubbed his toe on the nightstand. "Yeah, Rémy. Hang on a sec, okay?" He gave me a knowing glance and took the phone into the hall.

"How did you know it was Rémy?" Megan asked.

"I, uh, I saw the caller ID," I improvised. She frowned as she assessed the distance I was from the phone and the fact that my back was to it. Oops. We had so far managed to keep anything Seer-related from Megan, but she was obviously suspicious.

"Meg, can you get Ally a drink of water, please? From the kitchen?" Jack asked as he walked back into the bedroom and set the phone back on my nightstand. She gave him a long look before nodding and scooting off the bed. He waited until she was out of the room before addressing me. "You need to call him first thing in the morning, I told him we couldn't talk right now because of Meg." He sat beside me and took my hand.

"Thanks." I tried to smile. "How's your toe?"

"Fine. You'll tell me about it in the morning?"

"Of course." I leaned over to kiss him. "Sorry for the midnight drama."

"Here." Megan reappeared and handed me a glass of water. She took it from my hand when I was finished and set it on the nightstand. "You can sleep in the middle tonight, Ally. Jack and I will keep the nightmares away."

If only it were as simple as nightmares.

I called Rémy while Megan was in the shower the next morning. I had told Jack about the vision while he was getting ready for work. He hadn't said much, just kissed me fiercely and left.

"And you couldn't tell where you were? You recognized nothing?" Rémy asked.

"Nothing. It looked like some sort of abandoned building. It could be anywhere. Sorry."

"You have nothing to apologize for, cherié! You have no control over these damned visions. I know that."

"Yeah. Some gift, huh? I was searching for something. Something important. Ugh! Why are these visions so goddamn vague?"

"Calm down! Getting upset doesn't help, you know. We'll figure it out. Now, talk to Mina. She's been trying to grab the phone."

"Ally? Are you okay? We both woke up last

night, I guess when you had the vision. Oh, sweetie!"

"I'm fine, Mina. Thanks. When are you guys coming? I really miss you. Will you be here in time for the wedding?"

"Yes, definitely. We found out yesterday our bid was accepted." They were trying to buy the house across the street, catty-corner from ours. I had a "prophecy" soon after Jack and I returned from France that implied the chosen three needed to live in close proximity. "We're packing up this week. We should be there by early next week at the latest."

"Good. Can you bring my red dress? Listen, I have to go. Megan and I have a shopping date. I'll talk to you soon, okay?"

"All right. Give Megan and Jack our love. We'll see you soon."

Tara had decided to go with a 1950s vintage theme for her wedding. Megan and I stood on adjacent daises at the bridal shop, trying to be still lest the dressmaker's pins skewer us. The bridesmaids' dresses were a soft green, knee-length, with three-quarter sleeves and a boat neck. I felt like June Cleaver; all I needed was a string of pearls. Tara's dress was a breathtaking creation of ecru lace that looked amazing on her tall, lithe figure. After an hour of poking and prodding, I was heartily glad Jack and I had opted for a simple wedding. I was hosting a bridal shower for her on Sunday afternoon and the bachelorette party the following Friday. Jack was taking Mat out for a bachelor party the same night and the wedding was the following day.

"No! The neckline is all wrong! You promised you could do it like I asked!" Tara was in tears and the seamstress was at a loss.

"Okay, Bridezilla!" I hopped off my platform and put my arm around Tara, who was staring, horrified, in the 3-way mirror. "What is wrong with the neckline? It looks amazing."

"It does? Are you sure?"

"Positive. This neckline suits you and the dress style perfectly," I coaxed. "Now, go get changed so we can get some lunch. You always get cranky when your blood sugar crashes." She nodded and went off to change.

The seamstress whispered, "Thank you," and scurried to the back of the shop.

Tara calmed down once she had eaten a salad—she was convinced she needed to lose five pounds before the wedding—and was able to discuss the final preparations for her shower like a semi-sane person. "Has everyone RSVP'd? Do you have the games ready? How about the food?" Strike the semi-sane.

"Yes, to all of the above, Tara! You are going to be a basket case by the wedding!"

"What's a basket case?" asked Megan.

"A really crazy person, like Tara," I said. "This is exactly why Jack and I didn't have a big wedding."

She pushed the rest of her salad away and pouted. "I thought having a big wedding was important. You know I always wanted one." She looked at me and I nodded. She had always talked about and planned her dream wedding. "It's not as fun as I thought it would be. I'm stressed and nervous and driving Mat crazy. I don't think he even wants to get married anymore." Her eyes were shining again.

"Of course Mat wants to marry you!" Megan exclaimed. "He wants to *be* married, but no guy likes the *getting* married part."

We both stared at her. "You're right, Megan." Tara nodded.

"Out of the mouths of babes," I muttered.

"Okay, you're both right. As of now, I'm going to relax and let it go. It'll all happen just like it's supposed to. Right?" Tara asked worriedly.

"Yes, of course it will. Your mom is on it. Let her do the worrying. You need to just calm down and enjoy these last weeks before the wedding. Why don't you and Mat plan a getaway? Even if it's just overnight. You could go to Santa Fe," I suggested.

"Maybe," she mused. "I don't know."

"You should, Tara!" Megan urged. "You could ride the train."

Tara smiled fondly. "That's a great idea, sweetie. Thanks."

I started thinking it might be a good idea to plan a short getaway for Jack and me, as well; we hadn't had much time to ourselves since Megan had moved in. My husband and I needed a date night in the worst way. "Tara, what would you think about a double date? It's been ages, you know."

"Oh, my gosh! That would be great. Let's do it!" She bounced in her seat excitedly.

"Meg, can you stay with Trina and Manny this

weekend? Do you mind?" I asked.

"I don't mind, Ally." Of course not. She never minded anything.

***

I decided to surprise Jack with the double date. Megan got into the spirit of the deception, managing to keep it from Jack for three entire days. Trina was thrilled to have her for a couple nights and agreed to pick her up Friday afternoon before Jack got home from work. I packed a bag for Jack and me, including a new sexy little black lingerie set I figured he would appreciate and waited impatiently for him to get home.

"Ally? I'm home, hon."

I ran to him excitedly and threw myself in his arms, kissing him deeply.

"Mmm, what did I do to deserve this?" he asked.

"You had the good sense to marry me," I stated. We both laughed. "I have a surprise for you!"

"I like your surprises. What is it?"

"I'm kidnapping you! We're going to Santa Fe for the night with Mat and Tara. We're staying at La Fonda. What do you think? Are you surprised?"

"Very. I like it, as long as we have our own room," he teased.

"Of course. I'm not sharing you with anyone! Now, go take your shower because they'll be here in a few minutes. I've already packed for you."

"I take it Meg is at Trina's?"

"Yeah. I figured we needed some time to ourselves."

"You are a very wise woman." He kissed me and headed to the shower. "Give me five minutes."

We drove my SUV rather than take the train so we would be free to drive around Santa Fe if we wanted. The 60-mile trip to the state capitol took about an hour but passed quickly as we all caught up with each other. Tara was as good as her word and didn't mention anything about wedding plans; she and Mat seemed happier and more relaxed than they had for several weeks. We checked into the historic La Fonda Hotel on the Plaza and were given key cards to rooms across the hall from each other. We agreed to meet down in the lobby in half an hour to explore the plaza and find a place to eat dinner. Jack and I deposited our bags and left our room, eager to look at some of the artwork throughout the hotel. Well, I was eager and Jack was indulgent. I'd had a southwest art history class during my sophomore at UNM that had taught me about the history of La Fonda and how it had been a Fred Harvey hotel in the 1920s. I wanted to see the Gerald Cassidy paintings especially and hunted down four of them in the lobby, then proceeded to bore Jack with a running commentary. He nodded and made the appropriate noises, so I rewarded him with a good kiss when we found an out-of-the-way nook.

"Jeez, you two!" Tara interrupted us. "Give it a rest. I'm starving! Let's go find a place to eat."

"We'll get back to this later," Jack whispered.

"We'd better," I whispered back.

Tara rolled her eyes and led the way out the front doors. We found a bar and grill off the plaza that looked fun and smelled promising and headed upstairs to the restaurant. Jack and Mat each ordered a beer but Tara and I were both too young to order a glass of wine, something I found a bit difficult after living in France for a year where I had learned to appreciate good wine. You couldn't hang around Rémy for any time without drinking copious amounts of wine.

"Don't worry, babe. I grabbed a bottle from home before we left. We can have it later," Jack assured me.

"You're the best. Thank you." I leaned over and kissed his cheek.

We had an enjoyable dinner and then found a place with music and dancing for a few more hours. It was wonderful to relax and enjoy time with two of our best friends in the whole world. Our wedding had been so unexpected and then we had jumped right into parenthood, sort of. We hadn't had much of a chance to just be a young married couple and I was determined we would enjoy this brief chance to forget our responsibilities for a while.

After we had our fill of dancing and listening to the band, we walked back to our hotel and said goodnight to Tara and Mat, saying that we would see them the next morning for breakfast. Once in our room, I asked Jack to open the wine while I changed. I told him I had one more surprise for him and disappeared into the bathroom. We had only been married for two months and I hadn't had the chance, or the nerve, to wear sexy lingerie yet for my husband. Tara had told me that Mat loved it when she put on something sexy and I thought Jack would appreciate it too, but I didn't know if I could pull it off. Tara had taken me to Victoria's Secret and helped me pick out something not too extreme I thought I might be able to wear. Maybe. I sat on the commode, trying to work up the nerve to put on the lingerie. I have no idea why I was so nervous; he had seen me naked dozens of times, but this seemed different somehow. I finally mentally slapped myself for being such a chicken and donned the outfit. I peeked out the bathroom door to see where Jack was. He had poured the wine and was sitting on the edge of the bed, waiting for me.

"Ally?" he asked as he saw me peek out the door. "What's wrong, babe? Come out of the bathroom."

"Okay." I swallowed and made myself walk out and stand in front of my husband. "Surprise."

"Holy Mother of God."

"Do you like it? I kind of feel ridiculous."

"Why on earth would you feel ridiculous?" He pulled me to him, turning me around to get a fuller view. "You look hot! Wow. I love it. I feel like I just won the lottery."

"Really? I was worried," I admitted softly.

He smiled, seeming to understand that I was having a small confidence crisis. "Ally Ruiz, you are the most beautiful woman in the entire world to me. And I absolutely love this. But please don't feel like you have to wear sexy stuff just to make me happy. Wear it if you want, but only if you like it and it makes you feel good, okay?"

"Yeah. You're pretty awesome, you know that?"

"What? I wasn't paying attention because I'm

completely distracted by the sex goddess in front of me." We both laughed. He pulled me into his arms and we were done talking for quite a while.

Hours later I lay drowsing against his chest. "So, you're glad I kidnapped you tonight?"

"Definitely. We needed to get away for a little while. Ally." He turned to look at me. "How are you doing with all this? Is having Megan too much? Am I taking advantage of you?"

"Oh, Jack, no. Megan belongs with us. She is the easiest kid to have around. Too easy, sometimes. And you are not taking advantage of me. I am so happy. I love being married to you. Hey, we haven't even had a fight yet."

"Hmm, that's right. Maybe I should do something stupid so you can get mad at me. I've heard make-up sex is pretty great."

"Well, not right now, okay? I've got other plans for you." I began kissing his neck, letting my hands wander to all sorts of fun places.

"Are you trying to kill me, querida?" he asked with a groan.

I leaned back. "Well, we can't have that. Maybe I should stop."

He laughed and pulled me back. "No, don't stop. At least I'll die happy."

I had the vision/nightmare again that night. I jerked awake at the same point I did last time, when I was frantically searching for something, but managed to keep from screaming. If I was going to have to endure this thing repeatedly, as appeared likely, I could at least spare Jack the midnight drama. He worked too hard every day to skimp on his sleep. I lay as still as I could, trying to get my breathing back under control and wondering what I could possibly be searching for.

He rolled over and put his arm around me, pulling me into the cocoon of his body. "It's okay, babe. I've got you. I'm here," he mumbled sleepily against my hair.

I smiled and relaxed into his arms. He took care of me, even in his sleep.

Chapter Seven

"All men make mistakes, but a good man yields when he knows his course is wrong, and repairs the evil. The only crime is pride."
—Sophocles, *Antigone*

Mina and Rémy arrived on Monday; Tara, Megan, and I spent the entire day helping them unpack and get moved in. Jack and Mat came over as soon as they got home from work and between all of us we got them set up fairly well. They would need to shop for more furniture soon, but they had a place to sleep, at least. Finally, around 8:00 p.m., we ordered pizza and sat around, exhausted, while we ate and caught up.

"Tell us about the wedding," Tara suggested. "Was it wonderful?"

"Well, it was certainly big," Rémy said.

Mina gave him dirty look. "It was beautiful," she said. "Kate outdid herself. I have some pictures on my phone but the rest are still packed somewhere." She passed the phone around. She wore a gorgeous lace dress and smiled up at Rémy, who wore a tuxedo.

"You guys are gorgeous," I said. "It looks like it was a great party."

"It was. I wish you all could have been there. Do you have pictures from yours, Ally? And what about from Jack's graduation?" Mina asked.

I happily complied, sharing the photos from my own cellphone. We decided it was time to walk back across the street when we noticed Megan was asleep on the floor, her half-eaten piece of pizza still in her hand.

"Come on, munchkin," Jack scooped her up in his strong arms. "Let's get you to bed." She barely stirred as we worked together to wipe her face and tuck her in bed. "Your turn, querida." He scooped me up and carried me to our room, where he placed me on the bed. "You must be exhausted from helping Rémy and Mina all day. Would you like me to draw you a bath or give you a massage?"

"How can I possibly choose? What are my chances of getting both?" I teased.

"Better than average, I'd say. Don't move while I get that bath started."

I nearly fell asleep while he disappeared to get the bath going. He pulled me to my feet, led me to the bathroom, and undressed me before helping me into the tub. "Are you joining me?" I asked hopefully.

"Tempting, but no. Tonight I am treating my beautiful wife to a bath and a massage with no strings attached."

"Jack, I never think of our love life like that!" I

objected.

He leaned over to kiss me. "I know, babe. But I know you've worked hard all day and you're exhausted. Tonight is about you. Let me do this." I nodded and he poured me a glass of wine to drink while I soaked. What a totally amazing man! After my bath and a relaxing massage, we curled up together in bed and drank another glass of wine apiece.

"I'm going to miss you so much, Jack." He was leaving the day after the wedding for his obligatory two-week summer army training.

"I hate that I have to go. The timing sucks, I know. I'm sorry, Ally. You'll have to get Meg started at school and begin your student teaching while I'm gone."

"We'll be fine. Don't worry about us. I'm just not ready to let you go, to be separated again." I set my wine down and curled up tightly against his side.

He sighed. "Yeah, me neither."

I barely heard him as I was falling asleep.

***

"So, where are you taking Mat? Will there be strippers involved?" It was the night before the wedding and we had bachelor and bachelorette party responsibilities. Megan was staying with Trina and Manny.

Jack paused his shaving and laughed, meeting my eyes in the bathroom mirror. "Jesus, Ally! Strippers? No, hon. We're going to a sports bar to eat wings and watch a game. Strippers!" He laughed again and resumed shaving.

"Which sports bar?" What was wrong with me? I couldn't let it go.

"Probably Ojos Locos. Why?"

"That sleazy bar where the waitresses are half naked? I don't think so! You need to pick someplace else!" I crossed my arms and leaned against the cabinet.

He finished shaving and rinsed his razor. He crossed his arms and stared back at me. I could tell he was trying not to smile.

"You had better wipe that stupid smirk off your face, mister! I'm serious!"

He uncrossed his arms and put his hands on his hips. "Oh, yeah? You get to tell me what to do now?"

"I'm your wife!" I yelled like a jealous, psycho fishwife.

"Yeah, but you're not my keeper, Ally." He walked into the bedroom and got dressed silently while I remained stewing in the bathroom.

This was the first time since we got married that we were headed out for an evening away from each other and I was having issues apparently. I followed him to the front door. "Are you really going to take him to that bar?"

He stopped and ran his hands through his still-wet hair. "Yeah, I am. You have nothing to worry about. I love you, even when you're being ridiculous." He bent down to kiss me before he left.

To my shame, I didn't kiss him back.

***

"What the hell is wrong with you tonight?" Tara demanded as she stopped by our table between dances. "You're all depressed! You need to come out here and dance and have fun!" She tried to pull me out of my seat.

"I'm sorry." I was ruining the night for everyone. "Jack and I had a fight earlier. I was awful," I admitted.

"What did you fight about?" She plopped on the stool next to me. "Come on, Ally. Spill!"

I told her how I had thrown a fit about him taking Mat to Ojos Locos and demanded to know if they were going to see strippers.

"But we go there all the time. What's going on? Why are you suddenly so jealous? It's not like you, Ally."

"I know! What is my problem? I didn't even kiss him goodbye! What if he gets in a wreck on the way home? What if I never see him again?" I started hyperventilating.

"Mina!" Tara yelled at her across the dance floor.

"What's up?" Mina, flushed from dancing, trotted up to the table. They had both been enjoying themselves all evening while I moped and pouted at the table.

"Ally's in full freak-out mode. She and Jack had a fight," Tara explained.

Mina didn't waste any time; she reached for my wrist and put her other hand on my cheek, forcing me to meet her gaze. I felt her invade my mind as all my barriers dropped. Then I felt a calming influence flow through my thoughts as my breathing slowed to normal.

"How did you do that, Mina?" I asked in awe.

"I've been practicing. Oh, Ally. If you only knew how Jack feels about you. There is no reason in the world to be jealous." She pulled me close for a hug. "I think you're mainly upset about him leaving the day after tomorrow."

"I'm an idiot. I need to call him."

"Why don't you just text him? You can talk to him later. It's my bachelorette party and I want to enjoy it with my two best friends!" Tara exclaimed.

"Okay. Give me a minute." They both nodded and went back to the dance floor.

Me: I'm so so sorry. I'm a crazy person. Forgive me?

Jack: Of course. Always. Luv u. Talk to u later ok?

Me: Ok.

For the rest of the evening, I focused on making sure Tara's bachelorette party was fun. We went to several clubs and danced until we were exhausted. We ended the evening at the Frontier Restaurant across from the university and ate enormous cinnamon rolls swimming in butter sauce and drank coffee.

"After tomorrow, we'll all be married women," I observed.

"It's hard to believe, huh?" Tara said. "I never even wanted to go out with Mat. Now I can't imagine my life without him."

"I know what you mean," I agreed. "I hope I still fit into my dress after pigging out on this." I popped the last decadent bite in my mouth.

"Yeah, I'll probably need to barf it all up when I get home," Tara mused.

Jack was already home when I arrived. I literally threw myself in his arms and kissed him like I should have before he left, tasting beer and spicy wings. He wasn't much of a drinker, always limiting himself to one of anything because of his past. His mother had been killed by a drunk driver, his dad had turned into an alcoholic, and Jack himself had self-medicated with alcohol and drugs when he was much younger. "I'm so sorry I acted like a crazy, jealous bitch! I should never have tried to tell you what to do."

"It's okay, babe. I should have talked to you instead of reacting. And I shouldn't have laughed at you. I'm sorry too." He kissed me deeply, letting his warm tongue invade my mouth and tease my senses. "Hey, we've had our first fight. Good job on getting that out of the way, querida."

I laughed with him and then pulled him back for more kisses.

"Ally." He pulled away and held my face in his hands. "You don't have any reason to be jealous. I am only interested in you, I swear."

"I don't think I was really jealous, Jack. I'm just letting the two-week separation get to me, I guess. I'm so sorry." I told him what Mina had done to calm me down, amazed again at how her powers were developing.

"All right, enough apologizing. Let's put it behind us. Megan's not here and I have never had the opportunity to make love to my gorgeous wife in the middle of the living room. Or in the kitchen. I have extremely fond memories of almost making love to you once in your grandmother's kitchen and tonight I can make that particular fantasy come true."

"Well, it's pretty late, so if we're going to do all that we had better get busy."

***

"Ally, can I have my hair up too? Please?" Megan asked quietly. We were in the bride's room at the church waiting for Tara to arrive. She was late, of course.

I looked at Megan's long, shining black curls and wondered if I could manage a credible up-do for her. She so rarely asked for anything, so I wanted to try. "Sure, Meg. Sit down here and let me see what I can do." I brushed and braided her hair before coiling it tightly on top of her head and securing it with at least a dozen bobby pins. I shellacked it with multiple coats of hair spray and then stepped back to see what she thought. Her eyes met mine in the mirror as a lovely smile lit up her face. I caught a glimpse of the beautiful young woman she would become in a few short years and nearly gasped in awe. I don't know why it surprised me, given how good-looking her brother was. "You look gorgeous!"

"Thanks, Ally." She smiled and then turned to hug me tightly. She was an affectionate, but reserved child; she actually reminded me of Mina in a lot of ways. Jack and I both worried that she was growing up without a mother or a real father. We were trying to fulfill both roles, but we knew our youth handicapped us in some ways. I certainly didn't feel equipped for motherhood at age 20, but what could we do?

"Sorry I'm late!" Tara breezed in, looking stunning, holding an iced caramel macchiato.

"Seriously, Tara? You have twenty minutes until you're supposed to be walking down that aisle and you figured you had time to stop at Starbucks? Your wedding Nazi has been in here six times demanding to know where you are!" As I finished scolding her, Mina reappeared with the flustered wedding coordinator in tow. "She's here." I gestured to the late bride.

"Would you all relax?" Tara said as she took a sip of her coffee. "There's plenty of time. All I have to do is slip into the dress. My hair and makeup are done." She started shedding clothes as she finished. Her mother and grandmother came in just as she was stepping into the dress I held for her. Megan held back a giggle as her grandmother's eyes bugged out at the tiny thong and strapless bra Tara was wearing under her wedding gown. She sat down on the stool in front of the mirror while I helped her fasten the comb with the veil attached in her upswept blonde tresses. I got a little teary-eyed as I gazed at my best friend on her wedding day.

"Oh, no you don't!" she exclaimed and grabbed a tissue to dab at her eyes. "I just spent $200 for this makeup and hair. Knock it off!" She handed me a tissue as well, then hugged me. "Come on. I need to go marry Mat."

Less than five minutes later I was walking up the aisle toward a nervous-looking Mat. Jack, his best man, stood next to him, looking incredibly gorgeous in his grey tuxedo and tails. His vest and tie matched the bridesmaids' dresses perfectly. He watched me, smiling, until I reached the front of the church. I winked at him and turned to take my place. The minister motioned for the congregation to stand as the back doors of the church were opened to reveal Tara and her father. The music changed to the traditional wedding march and they started up the aisle. I glanced over at Mat and had to bite my lip at the expression on his face: pure, unadulterated love. It was clear to everyone in the church that Mat felt like the luckiest man in the world today. They exchanged vows they had written themselves before the minister told Mat he could kiss his bride. They grinned at each other before he pulled her into his arms for their first kiss as Mr. and Mrs. Mateo Jimenez. I wiped away yet another tear and looked up to see Jack smiling at me. *I love you,* he mouthed. Mat and Tara reluctantly pulled away from each other and walked back down the aisle and out of the church. I walked forward to meet Jack. He tucked my arm under his and patted my hand.

"You okay, babe?"

"Yeah. I'm happy, that's all."

We collected Megan and drove ten minutes north to the Sandia Casino Resort, on the Sandia Indian Reservation, just outside Albuquerque. The members of the wedding party and the family were required to pose for approximately a thousand photographs on the gorgeous resort grounds, with the majestic Sandia Mountains in the background. Tara's wedding album was sure to be stunning. After a delicious buffet dinner, I danced with my husband and then my new cousin-in-law at the reception, while Jack danced with Tara. I sat out while he danced with his little sister and got a lump in my throat watching them. *We would make it work,* I vowed silently. *We would somehow be the parents Megan needed us to be.* Jack returned to sit beside me while Megan danced with Mat.

"We're all old married folks now," he said as he put his arm around the back of my chair.

"Yeah. I wonder how long it'll be until one of us pops out a kid," I mused.

"Please say it won't be us anytime soon," he begged. I had to smile at the utter panic evident on his face.

"I have no plans to get pregnant in the near future, don't worry. I kinda think we've got our hands full with Megan right now."

"Whew! I am not ready for a baby."

"Me neither, hon." I leaned into him. "I would really like to graduate from college and start my career before we even think about having more kids."

We stayed until nearly the bitter end, through the cake, bouquet toss—which Megan caught—the garter fling, which Jack and Mat's young cousin, Javier, caught, and all the toasts.

Jack gave the first toast and talked about how Mat was so much more than a cousin: he was his best friend and a brother. He was glad Mat had the good sense to marry Tara, his own wife's best friend. We all had a laugh as he tried to sort out his pronouns, but he ended by claiming all the credit for getting them together by setting them up on a blind date. When it was my turn, I claimed the credit for them getting together, completely discrediting Jack's matchmaking attempts and retelling the story of their disastrous first date. Everyone laughed and I ended by offering my toast and leaning over to kiss my own husband. Even I had to admit it was pretty adorable that the best man and matron of honor were married.

Tara and Mat were spending their wedding night there in the hotel before leaving the next morning for a week in Cancun at an all-inclusive resort, which sounded like something Jack and I definitely needed to check out sometime. The thought of having a vacation that didn't include anything Seer-related seemed like a dream come true.

"What are you smiling about?" Jack pulled me close and twirled me as we danced again.

"I'm just imaging you and me on a Mexican resort beach, that's all."

"Mmm, sounds great. Do we have clothes on?" he whispered in my ear.

I laughed. "It's not that kind of beach, Jack!"

"Shoot. Well, it sounds pretty good, anyway. Maybe next summer we could do that."

"Let's definitely keep it in mind. We better get Megan home soon. You have to get up pretty early too."

"Yeah, she's starting to droop and I'm ready to have you to myself." He nibbled my ear as he finished. "You look amazing tonight. I don't think I've had a chance to tell you that yet."

"Thanks. You look pretty spiffy yourself in a tux. I hope the pictures we took with Megan earlier turn out well. Our first family picture," I mused.

He leaned down and kissed me fully, something he didn't often do in public. "Thank you for saying that, querida. You have no idea what it means to me."

"I kind of think I do, but that's not why I said it." I laid my head against his chest and we finished the song.

***

He tried to go without waking me the next morning, but I felt him leave the bed and I got up to see him off, assuring him I would go back to sleep as soon as he was gone. That proved impossible and I sat on the back patio drinking coffee until Megan woke up. We spent the day moping and watching Disney movies, already missing Jack. We finally roused ourselves late in the afternoon because my mom had invited us for dinner.

"So, what have you heard about your student teaching?" my mom asked as she cut Elijah's chicken for him.

"Where Jack?" my little brother demanded. He

was not even slightly interested in his dinner and was squirming to get down from the table. Jack was his favorite, mainly because he played rougher with him than any of the rest of us, tossing him in the air any time the toddler tugged at his pant legs. Jack had endless patience with him, probably because of all the practice he had with the multitude of young cousins in his family.

"I told you, Eli! He's at the army." Megan rolled her eyes at me. Elijah had been demanding to know where Jack was since we walked in the door.

I smiled at her in sympathy before answering my mother. "I got a placement, finally. I'll be at Eldorado High School. I go later this week to meet with my cooperating teacher."

"Oh, good. I was starting to get worried. And what about you, Miss Megan? Have you met your teacher, yet?"

She shook her head. "When do we go, Ally?"

"Tuesday. We'll go in the morning and then we can go shopping for all your school supplies. What kind of backpack do you want this year?"

She shrugged and appeared to think about it.

"You may need to take out a loan to pay for school supplies, you know. I can't believe how long the lists are these days," Brian grumbled. "Elijah's preschool list was ridiculous!"

"Well, if the state would stop cutting funding to the schools—" my mom began.

"Great, Brian. You had to get her started," I said.

"When you have your own classroom you'll care about funding too," she argued.

"I know, Mom, I know. This is great macaroni

and cheese. Is it a new recipe?" I desperately tried to change the subject away from one of her favorite rants.

She narrowed her eyes at me. "Nice try, Ally. Fine, I'll keep my unwanted opinions to myself. Who wants dessert?" She stood up and stalked to the kitchen. Brian and I met each other's gaze guiltily.

"Where Jack?" Elijah demanded yet again, oblivious to the adult tension in the room.

Ah, family. I loved mine fiercely, but nothing could frustrate me more at times.

***

Megan surprised me by eschewing the plastic Disney backpacks and choosing a regular one with multicolored polka dots. "Mikayla and I decided we should be more grown up this year. We are 5th graders, you know," she said seriously.

I valiantly held back an indulgent smile and agreed with her solemnly. "You probably want a grown-up lunchbox too, huh?"

"Definitely. Will you help me find a good one? I don't want to look like a baby this year."

"Of course I will." We had attended the meet-and-greet with her new teacher earlier that morning and then headed off to shop for all the school supplies on the lengthy list.

"This stuff costs a lot, huh?" Megan asked worriedly. "I don't need a new lunchbox."

It had all added up quickly, but Trina and Brian had both slipped me some cash to help pay for all of

Megan's school expenses, plus my dad still deposited a healthy sum into my account each month. Jack got a stipend from the army and worked as many hours as possible at the body shop, so we were doing fine financially. We had decided it would be better if I didn't work while I was doing my student teaching, especially since Megan was with us now. We didn't want her to spend hours in after-school care every day.

"Oh, Meg, please don't worry about it. It's fine. Of course you need a new lunch box. Let's check at Home Goods. I saw some there last week. We have just enough time before we meet Grams for lunch."

Grams was waiting for us when we arrived at Savory Fare, a local lunch spot specializing in fresh salads and interesting sandwiches. Grams and I ordered the salad of the day, fresh greens with crispy goat cheese medallions, while Megan settled on grilled cheese, her all-time favorite, with tomato-basil soup.

"Now, catch me up on everything that has been happening this summer," Grams commanded. "I haven't seen near enough of you since you and Jack got married!"

"I've missed you too, Grams. I want to have you over for dinner, maybe later this week?"

"That would be lovely," she replied, so we planned to have her come for taco night Thursday, which was Megan's other favorite. It was hard to mess up tacos, especially if Megan helped me cook.

***

I dropped Megan at Mikayla's house the next morning for a few hours of playtime while I drove to the high school to meet the supervising teacher I would be working with for the next school year. I was nervous, knowing this first impression was important. The parking lot was overflowing due to student registration, so I had to park quite a distance away and was afraid I was running late for our meeting. It took several more minutes to find my way across the unfamiliar campus to the classroom I was looking for in the H building. I arrived at room 7, breathless and sweaty, and knocked on the open door before walking in and approaching the teacher's desk.

"Mr. Harris? Hi, I'm Ally Moran. I mean Ruiz." I was nervous and stuttered over my new last name like an idiot. I had considered hyphenating instead of totally changing my last name to take Jack's, but in the end it seemed like a lot of trouble.

The man behind the desk looked to be maybe in his late forties, with a gorgeous head of silver-black hair. He glanced up and smiled distractedly, yet kindly. "Nice to meet you. Are you going to be in my AP lit class this year? You're here for the reading list, of course." He began shuffling through piles of papers on his messy desk.

Yeah, I get that a lot because of my height, or lack thereof. I had tried to dress professionally this morning, but I guess it didn't help. "Um, no. I'm actually your new student teacher."

"Oh, of course. Forgive me. Miss Ruiz, was it?" He stood up and came forward to shake my hand. "Sorry about that."

I shook his hand. "It's *Mrs*. Ruiz. Ally. Nice to meet you."

He looked surprised, but at least tried to cover it. "Nice to meet you too. Have a seat and we'll get you set up." He had cleared a spot for me at a table near his and provided me with a syllabus and copies of the textbooks he used. "I have two sections of Advanced Placement Language and Literature this year and three sections of regular English 12. Here's the reading list." He handed me a sheet of paper with a lengthy selection of novels, short stories, and poems. "Any that you're not familiar with, you should get started reading. I've got copies of all the novels."

I was happy to see that most of it was familiar; the only drama I hadn't studied was *Antigone* and the only new novel was a Willa Cather story, *O Pioneers!*. I looked up from my perusal of the list to find him leaning against his desk and smiling apologetically at me.

"I'm so sorry I confused you with a student. I didn't mean to get us off on the wrong foot. I was expecting you, but then I got caught up in my work and you took me by surprise. Plus, you do look really young. Sorry, you probably hate that, but it's true. Can I ask how old you are without completely offending you?"

I laughed lightly. "It's fine. I get it, Mr. Harris." I shrugged. "I'm 20."

"Charlie, please. We're colleagues. Wow, you are young. I have children older than you. And you're married? Do you have kids?" To his credit he winced as he said this, as if he didn't mean to ask if I got knocked up and had to get married.

"No, but my husband and I are raising his ten year old sister."

"Oh my goodness. You have your hands full. Well, let me introduce you to some of the other English teachers around here." He walked me around to the nearby classrooms to meet the rest of the teachers in our department, then took me around the corner to what was obviously the foreign language department, judging by all the posters and signs in French, German, and Spanish. He led me to a room that had 'Madame Harris' on the door. "I want you to meet my wife." We walked in to find a lovely woman about Charlie's age, standing on a stepladder to hang some posters. "Let me do that, Camille." He held out his hand to help her down. "Come down and meet Ally, my new student teacher."

"Ah, Charlie, you are always so sweet!" She was obviously French and greeted me with "Bonjour" and a *faire la bise,* kissing my cheeks like Rémy always did.

"Bonjour," I said, returning the kisses. *"Comment allez vous?"*

She looked surprised, yet delighted, and lobbed a couple more phrases at me. Realizing I was fluent, she launched into a full-on conversation in French, while Charlie stood by, looking bemused.

"Well, you've made her day," he commented as we returned to his classroom. "She doesn't get the chance to speak French here in Albuquerque as much as she would like. Where did you learn to speak so well?"

"I spent last year in France on an exchange, plus I'm minoring in it."

"Well, you should get your certification in it, as well. Make yourself as marketable as possible as you begin your job search," he advised. "It's not always easy to get a job as an English teacher, unfortunately. It seems like math and science teachers are all that's wanted these days."

"Tell me about it! My husband is studying engineering and he's had all kinds of offers of jobs. It doesn't seem fair."

He chuckled. "No, it certainly doesn't. How much longer does your husband have until he graduates? Has he thought about where to work?"

"He graduated in May but he's starting his master's degree this fall. He's in the army, so he will owe them a few years after his graduate work," I explained.

We wrapped up our initial meeting as I realized I was due to pick Megan up soon. He told me he would see me the following Tuesday, when school started.

***

High school started at 7:30 a.m. while elementary school didn't start until 8:00, so Trina would be taking Megan to school until Jack returned. I finished at 2:30, so I should be able to pick her up each day. My first day of student teaching included introducing myself to each of the classes and then sitting and observing how Charlie got the school year started. I took copious notes, knowing I would have assignments based on them as soon as my classes started at the university. There had been an orientation meeting for all the student teachers and we had a companion class this semester. I also had a couple other classes to wrap up the rest of my degree and my French minor, so it would be an intense semester. I was walking into the teacher's lounge for lunch when I was stopped by another teacher and informed that students were not allowed inside. Sigh. I patiently showed her my faculty ID tag and explained that I was a student teacher. She was embarrassed and apologized, but I realized I would face this kind of thing a lot in the foreseeable future. The teachers were welcoming and I found a group of younger teachers that I connected with pretty well, so I was hopeful that this year would be at least somewhat fun.

After I finished my day I drove by Megan's school to pick her up, pulling my SUV into the long line of parents waiting to pick up their kids. I thought back fondly to the first time Jack and I spoke, in our junior year of high school. He had helped me when I had my first-ever vision and then had driven me home in his Mustang, stopping to pick Megan up at this same school. This would be her last year here, and then she would have to brave the horror of middle school. I spotted her as she walked out, looking adorable in the outfit we had chosen for her first day. She walked beside a blonde, curly-headed boy, probably a classmate, chatting and laughing, which pleased me because she was usually so reticent. Maybe she had made a new friend. I looked closer at the boy as they neared the line of cars. He was shorter than Megan, who was not at all tall for her age, and appeared solemn. He had such a serious, almost sad, look on his face and it struck me for some reason. Had I seen him before? I got one of those feelings I get that he was going to be important somehow. I shivered slightly, realizing that it wasn't an entirely positive feeling. I'd had a similar feeling the first time I ever saw Jack, but it had been completely positive in his case, accompanied by a healthy dose of attraction, which had caused me to choose an empty desk in front of him, rather than in the front of the classroom, which was where I usually sat.

"Who was that?" I asked as she climbed in the back seat. She had at least two more years until I would allow her to ride in the front seat with the airbag.

"That's Kai. He's new this year 'cause he just moved here. Some kids were making fun of him 'cause he talks kinda funny, so I told them to stop. Kai's my friend now," she stated flatly.

My heart melted at her defense of a new boy who apparently had a speech impediment. She was so much like Jack sometimes; chivalry ran deep in the Ruiz veins. "That's great, Meg. Maybe you can invite him over some afternoon."

"Thanks, Ally. I'm glad you and Jack got married. I like living with you."

"Ah, sweetie, thanks. I like living with you too. Now, you buttered me up really good, so why don't we stop for gelato to celebrate our first day of school?"

She giggled and agreed.

***

Jack was due back in less than an hour and Megan and I were frantically trying to put the finishing touches on the welcome home picnic we had planned. We were setting out tiki torches and stringing lights on the back patio; I knew he was always exhausted when he returned from these two-week training exercises and I liked to have dinner waiting for him. It was tempting to farm Megan out for the night so we could have some alone time, but she had missed her big brother too.

He let himself in forty-five minutes later and Megan launched herself at him. "Hey, Squirt." He picked her up and gave her a tired hug. I took her place and kissed him tenderly. "God, I missed you both so much." He sighed into my hair.

"We missed you too. You look exhausted, Jack." I pulled away and led him toward our bedroom. "Get a shower and then we have a surprise picnic dinner for you outside. I've had a steak marinating for you all day."

"That sounds great, babe. Thanks. The food really sucked at camp this year."

He joined us on the patio ten minutes later, freshly showered but unshaven in a sexy, scruffy way I loved. I handed him an ice-cold beer and directed him to sit; he was not allowed to do any of the cooking tonight. Megan set out the side dishes while I grilled a giant steak for Jack, a much smaller one for Megan, and a portabella mushroom for myself. I might be a vegetarian, but I could manage to cook a decent steak as long as I paid attention and didn't walk away from the grill. The picnic was a great success and we all watched a movie together afterward, although Jack snored lightly through most of it.

Later, once Megan was asleep, I grabbed a quick shower and then joined Jack in our bed, where he was catching up on Facebook on his iPad. He set it aside as I lifted the covers to crawl in and pulled me next to him.

"This is what I've been looking forward to," he said as he kissed me deeply.

"Are you sure you're not too tired?" I asked, skimming my hands across his scruffy jaw.

"I'm never too tired for this."

***

We enjoyed the weekend together, the three of us, lounging around and then spending Sunday afternoon with Jack's extended family at Manny and Trina's, celebrating the end of summer. The university had another week until it started, so Jack worked at the body shop all week, getting in a good number of hours before his graduate classes curtailed his work schedule. I was getting settled in with my student teaching and Megan seemed happy with her teacher and her new classmates, once she had put them in their place about making fun of Kai's speech impediment. She was a quiet kid, but I could tell that she was viewed as a leader among her peers.

I drove into the pickup lane after school on Tuesday to find her, as usual, talking and laughing with Kai. She said something to him and then ran over to the car.

"Ally, can Kai come over today? Please?" she asked.

"Um, I don't know, sweetie. I think we should plan for that." Her little face fell. Crap. I hated disappointing her, and she truly asked for so little. "I mean, he needs to get permission from his parents—"

"What if he calls his dad? You could talk to him, Ally. Please? We want to work on a project together."

Great. Throw that in. What kind of future teacher refuses to let kids work on a project? "Well, if I can talk to his dad, I guess it might be okay."

"Yay! Thanks, Ally." She turned and motioned for the little boy to approach. "Call your dad. If he says it's okay, you can come over. But my sister wants to talk to him."

She closed the deal when she called me her sister. I smiled encouragingly at Kai. "Hi. I'm Ally. If you can get permission from your dad, it's okay if you come home with us."

"I'll call my nanny. My father doesn't like me to disturb him at work," the boy said quietly.

He didn't have a speech impediment at all; he had an accent. He was clearly English, but not with the sort of accent I had heard on the *Harry Potter* movies. His sounded less cultured, somehow, like maybe he was from an uneducated background. I felt horrible for thinking it, but at the same time I had a feeling there was something about it I was supposed to remember, but couldn't call to the front of my mind. He spoke on his cell phone—who gives a 5th grader a cell phone?—for a moment before handing it to me.

The woman on the other end introduced herself as Kai's nanny and said he had her permission to go home with us. When I asked if she would like our address so she could pick him up later, she said he was fine walking home. Before I had a chance to object, she had hung up. I handed the phone back to the boy, who took it stoically before climbing into the backseat with Megan. She chattered all the way home about how she would show him her dog and her cat—she had claimed Wicky as her own from the moment she moved in—and her bedroom. I wondered what the protocol was for letting her have a boy in her bedroom; Jack and I had never discussed it, assuming it wouldn't come up at her age. I felt completely out of my depth.

Once back at the house, the two children disappeared into the backyard so Kai could be introduced to Sodapop while I headed to the kitchen to see what I could find in the way of a snack for them. After eating apple slices with peanut butter and glasses of milk, they were planning to look on the Internet for ideas for their science project. I set up my laptop for them in the den and checked on them from time to time. Megan was in charge of the computer and Kai sat beside her with seeming endless patience as they searched for an idea they could both get interested in. He hadn't said anything to me since handing me his phone earlier except 'thank you' when I placed his snack in front of him. He had startling green eyes that looked sad and serious, like he had seen too much in his short life, but as he watched Megan search on the computer, I saw him smile slightly, as if he had found a great treasure. My heart went out to the small, lonely boy and I determined that I would welcome him into my home whenever possible.

Jack got home and was duly introduced to Kai before they disappeared into Megan's bedroom. I caught her before she ran off and leaned down to whisper in her ear to leave the door open. She looked at me questioningly, but nodded before skipping off.

"What's that all about?" Jack asked as he pulled me into his arms for a hello kiss.

"Megan has a new friend," I said before leaning into him for another kiss. As I pulled away, I saw Kai watching us from the hallway. Our eyes met, then he turned and followed Megan. Okay, that was a little creepy. When I peeked into her bedroom a little while later, they were sitting on the floor with a collection of small toys in between them. "What are you guys doing?"

"Just playing," Megan said. Kai didn't speak.

"Oh, okay. Kai, would you like to stay for dinner?"

"No, ma'am. Thank you. I better get home. See you tomorrow, Megan," he said quietly and stood to leave.

"I can drive you home, Kai. I don't want you to have to walk."

"No, thank you. I'm fine. It's not far." He gathered his backpack and left quietly, waving to Megan as he walked down the path to the sidewalk.

Chapter Eight

"Then reflect, my son: you are poised, once more, on the razor-edge of fate."
—Sophocles, Antigone

I ran. Tripped and fell, cutting my hands and knees on broken glass. Cried out. I picked myself up and ran again. Searching, crying out. "Megan? Where are you? Megan, please!" I searched frantically, my heart breaking as I couldn't find her. Someone was up ahead, crouched on the ground, amidst broken bottles and litter. It was a teenage boy, maybe 14 or 15 years old. His back was to me, shoulders hunched as he wept, his dark blonde curls shaggy and overly long. I wasn't afraid to approach him; I somehow knew he would have the answers I sought. I crept toward him, looking wildly around. I placed my hand on his thin shoulder and he turned his ravaged face toward me, tears streaming out of his piercing green eyes. "I'm sorry, Ally. I didn't want this. She isn't part of this. I tried to save her, but he made me! I'm so sorry!" I backed away,

shaking my head, starting to sob. Megan! Oh, my
God, where was she? What had happened to her?

"Ally, hon, wake up."

I woke to Jack gently shaking me and rubbing my back. "What?" I reached up to find my face wet with tears. My pillow was a soggy mess.

"Bad dream?" he asked. "You were crying in your sleep."

"Oh, God, Jack," I curled into his embrace and told him about the new additions to my dream/vision. "It's Megan! She's what I was looking for! She's in danger, Jack! She's in danger because of me!"

"Hey, hey," he soothed. "You don't know that. These visions of yours are always vague. We'll protect her, Ally. I won't let anything happen to her. I won't let anything happen to you, either."

I wanted to believe him, but I couldn't help remembering Michael. He had been killed because of me. Maybe it wasn't safe to be around me. I knew I wasn't thinking clearly right now in the middle of the night, but it was difficult to think about anything else. I curled deeper into Jack's chest, breathing in his comforting smell as he stroked my hair.

"We're going to figure this out, babe. I swear. I will not let anything threaten my family," he promised.

"But, Jack, what if—"

"Shh. It's no good trying to figure it out tonight."

"It's me, Jack." I sobbed into his chest. "I'm not safe. Everyone around me is in danger. I should—"

"Don't even go there!" He forced me to look into his eyes. "We tried that and it just about killed me. We belong together and we're a family now. Please, Ally. Please don't even think about leaving. We can figure out anything else. You are my life. You and Meg. I don't even want to think about life without you."

"I'm so sorry, Jack," I whispered. "I'm sorry about everything. You should have someone who's normal."

He laughed and pulled me to lie on top of him. "Oh, Ally! What's normal?" I knew he was trying to lighten the mood and I appreciated his effort.

"I don't know, but probably not a wife who has terrifying visions and has a murderer trying to control her." I smiled crookedly as I looked into his face. He was my life too, and I couldn't imagine being happy without him.

"Hey, your visions are what brought us together, so they don't bother me in the least. As far as Luc goes—well, we're going to find him and take care of him." The look on his face was so fierce; I was reminded that although he was studying to be an engineer, he was also a trained warrior, capable of killing with his bare hands, not to mention highly trained in all sorts of weapons I didn't even want to think about.

I lowered my lips to his, intent on taking our minds off the nightmare for now. "I love you so much, Jack. You and Megan are my life too. I'm not going anywhere." I kissed him again, then squirmed off of him and out of bed. "Except over here to lock the door. I wouldn't want Megan to interrupt what we're about to do."

"Oh, yeah? And what are we about to do, Mrs. Ruiz? I have no idea what you're talking about," he teased, the earlier fear and tension forgotten for the night.

I shut and locked our bedroom door, quietly, hoping that Megan was still fast asleep. I turned and stood for a moment, watching my husband as he sat up in bed. "I love being married to you, Jack."

He smiled and held out his hand to me. "Why don't you come over here so I can show you how much I love being married to you too?"

I happily complied.

***

I smelled coffee when I woke the next morning and was confused, since Jack was still asleep beside me. I threw on a robe and padded out to the kitchen. "Megan, did you make coffee, sweetie?"

Megan wasn't in the kitchen. Instead, Rémy looked up from his iPad and gestured to the cup of coffee he had poured for me.

I picked it up, took a sip, and grumpily muttered something about needing to change the locks as soon as possible.

"Always so cranky in the morning, eh, cherié? Maybe Jack isn't doing a good job of making your nights enjoyable," he said and smirked into his coffee cup.

"You're a pig, Rémy," I said it more out of habit than anything else; this back-and-forth banter was our way of communicating. "Thanks for the coffee.

What's up? Why are you here so early? " It wasn't even 6:00 a.m. yet.

"I wanted to hear about the vision. Mina wouldn't let me call last night. She said you wouldn't want to be disturbed."

I felt my cheeks heat up as I remembered the night before, after the dream. It was tough having Mina and Rémy in my head sometimes.

"Maybe there's hope for Jack after all," he said.

"Shut up! Do you want to hear about the vision or not?"

"That's why I'm here, cherié."

Jack came in while I was telling Rémy about the vision. He didn't say anything, but began preparing scrambled eggs for breakfast. He placed a plate in front of me and offered one to Rémy, who waved it away.

"No, thank you. Mina has breakfast waiting for me at home. I just wanted to hear about the dream before Ally left for work. Do you have any idea who the boy was? One of your students, perhaps?"

"No, but I feel like I should know." I shook my head, frustrated. "It's just out of reach."

"Rémy!" Megan squealed as she entered the kitchen and saw one of her favorite people. He bent down and kissed both her cheeks, which she loved. "Where's Mina? Did you come for breakfast? "

"No, love. I just stopped by to make some coffee for your brother. I figured he had to be sick of Ally's by now. Mina is still at home."

She giggled and hugged him before plopping down at the table to eat the plate of eggs and toast Jack had prepared for her.

***

I wasn't surprised to find Kai walking to the car with Megan later that afternoon; I had a feeling this would become a pattern and I was glad Megan had found a friend, even though I found the boy disturbing somehow.

"Kai's nanny said it was okay if he came home with us. Is it okay, Ally?" Megan asked as they climbed in the car.

Short of booting him out of my car, the decision seemed to have already been made. "Sure. No problem." It occurred to me that Kai's nanny didn't do much nanny-ing. "Are you guys going to work on your science project?"

"Yeah. Jack said that he'd help us tonight. We're going to do a project on how to reduce fiction," she stated.

"Friction," Kai whispered to her.

"Well, if Jack's helping you it had better be 'friction.' If it's 'fiction,' I can help you, but we certainly don't want to *reduce* fiction." Megan and I both laughed, but Kai merely smiled. What a serious, sober little guy!

We got home and they disappeared while I fixed them a snack—mini pizza bagels—that Megan wolfed down, but Kai stared at suspiciously before finally tasting. He must have found it agreeable because it quickly disappeared.

"Thanks for putting pepperoni on them, Ally," she said, then addressed Kai. "Ally's a vegetarian, but Jack and me love meat."

"Jack and I," I corrected.

"She's also an English teacher," Megan rolled her eyes.

"Kai, would you like another bagel?" I asked. He was too thin and small for his age and I found I had a previously unknown maternal streak that wanted to fatten him up a bit.

"Thank you, ma'am," he said quietly and looked up to meet my questioning gaze.

I nearly dropped the plate of pizza bagels. I recognized those green eyes! They were the same eyes that had stared at me in my nightmare/vision last night! But they had stared at me from an older version of the young boy now sitting at my kitchen table.

"Ally, are you okay? You look funny. Why are you staring at Kai?" Megan looked between the two of us like she was watching a ping-pong match.

Kai broke the staring contest and reached for another bagel. I set the plate down on the table and turned back toward the refrigerator, ostensibly to get the milk. *Rémy! Rémy! Are you home? Can you hear me?* There was no response and I knew I wasn't getting through. It felt like I was hitting a brick wall, like my thoughts were being hemmed in somehow. I tried again, but it was the same thing. I looked at the two children to see Megan chewing and chattering to Kai while he stared at his plate. As if he felt me looking at him, he raised his eyes to mine slowly. There was a strange, knowing expression in his eyes. Weird. I poured them each another glass of milk and excused myself. I grabbed my purse and retreated to my bedroom to call Rémy on my cellphone.

"Cherié, you pick the worst times to call, do you know that?" I could hear Mina giggling in the background.

"It's three o'clock in the afternoon, Rémy! Jeez!"

"So? There is a proper time?"

"Whatever. Listen, if you could tear yourself away from your amorous pursuits for a few minutes, I would like you to come over here. Megan's new friend just so happens to be the boy I saw in my vision last night, except he was a lot older in the dream. Plus, I just tried to communicate with you mentally and couldn't get through at all. It didn't feel like you were blocking me, either. It was different."

He sighed. "All right. Give me few minutes to get dressed and I'll be over."

"Wow. Way too much information." I could hear him laughing as he hung up.

He let himself in five minutes later, carrying a plate covered with aluminum foil. "Mina made cookies this morning and wanted me to bring you some."

"Rémy!" Megan dropped her bagel remnant and jumped up from her seat to give him a hug, probably depositing pizza sauce on his expensive shirt. He hugged her back with one arm while handing me the plate of cookies with the other. "This is Kai." She presented her friend as if he were an unusual specimen she had found. "Kai, this is Rémy. He and Mina live across the street. He's from *France*." She said it as if it were a magical realm.

"Bonjour, Kai." Rémy held out his hand to the boy. "It is a pleasure to meet you."

Kai stared at Rémy's outstretched hand and took a small step backward. "Hello," was all he said as he put his own hands in his pockets.

Rémy dropped his hand and raised his eyebrows at me. He addressed me in French. "Interesting child. Are you sure about him being in your vision?"

I answered back in French, not wanting Kai and Megan to understand us. "Positive. This is really weird. And do you see what I mean about us being blocked? I can't get through to you at all."

"No, nor I. What do you make of it?"

"I don't know. Do you think it has anything to do with the boy?" I asked.

"He's only a child. I don't see how it could."

"Why are you guys talking in French?" Megan asked, hands on her little hips.

"Oh, were we?" Rémy smiled at her. "*Pardon, mon petit chou.* I didn't even realize."

She glared at him suspiciously. "What does that mean? What did you just call me?"

"It means 'my little cabbage,' but the French say it all the time," I explained. "Why don't you and Kai go play in your room for a while?"

"Come on, Kai. They want to get rid of us so they can talk." She took him by the hand and led him away.

"What do you know about this boy?" Rémy continued in French.

"Nothing at all. He's new this year, obviously English. Megan says the other kids were making

143

fun of him because of his accent. He has a nanny who doesn't seem to do much. She never picks him up from school and makes him walk home from our house."

"She may not have an American driver's license," he pointed out. "What's his last name? I could do a little checking."

"I don't know. I'll find out from Meg and get back to you. Do you and Mina want to come over for dinner?"

"That sounds nice. Thanks. We'll bring dessert," he offered.

"You already did." I gestured to the plate of cookies.

Jack arrived home and helped the two children with their science project while I put the finishing touches on dinner. Kai again refused my offer to stay and eat with us, shouldered his backpack, and left quietly.

I had called Tara and Mat to come over as well, and we made it an impromptu barbecue party. I added some ice cream to go along with Mina's wonderful chocolate macadamia nut cookies and threw together some macaroni and cheese to go with the steaks Jack grilled. Tara brought a vegetarian potato salad, which was a thoughtful addition for her vegetarian best friend. I was anxious to see their honeymoon pictures as this was the first time we'd had a chance to get together since the wedding. Looking at the gorgeous pictures of them on the beach made me even more resolute to look into that resort for next summer. Maybe we could take Megan for a family vacation at the start of the summer.

We waited until Megan was off taking her bath and getting ready for bed to have a conference about the recent developments with my nightmare/visions.

"Do you realize that we can communicate now?" I asked Mina and Rémy. Both nodded. "Maybe it does have something to do with Kai. This worries me. Should I keep Megan from playing with him? Should I let him into our home?"

"I have a hard time believing a small child could have anything to do with blocking our thoughts," Mina said softly.

"Always so soft-hearted." Rémy lifted her hand and kissed it. "I've never heard of a child having any power like that, but that doesn't mean it couldn't happen."

"So, you think I should keep Megan away from him?" I asked.

"On the contrary." He stood up and poured another glass of wine. "You've heard the saying 'keep your friends close and your enemies closer'?"

"How could a little kid be an enemy?" Jack asked.

"I don't know," Rémy mused. "But I have a feeling that things are beginning to happen. We must be ready."

***

My phone buzzed during lunch the next day. I was sitting in the teacher's lounge having a lively conversation in French with Camille Harris, planning a Saturday lunch outing with her, Mina, and Rémy to a local French restaurant she raved about. I saw that it was Megan's school and I excused myself to answer, tendrils of dread creeping over me; this couldn't be good. It wasn't. Apparently Megan was sitting in the principal's office because she got in a fight. I told Charlie I had to go, which he was super nice about, and I drove to the elementary school, sure there must be a mistake. There was absolutely no way my sweet sister-in-law would ever get in a fight! She was sitting dejectedly in a straight-backed chair along the wall of the office, her blouse and jeans torn, her face dirty and tear-streaked. Kai sat beside her looking even worse, with a rapidly blackening eye and a bloody nose he was holding a tissue against. They were holding hands so I assumed they had not fought with each other.

"Meg! Sweetie, are you okay? What happened?" I rounded the secretary's desk and knelt in front of her.

She threw herself in my arms and clasped my neck tightly. "I'm sorry, Ally! I didn't mean to."

"Okay, okay," I soothed and pulled back to brush the hair out of her face. "Tell me what happened."

"They were making fun of Kai and me, saying horrible, nasty things. I told them to stop, but then one of the boys, Tyler, pushed me and I fell and ripped my pants and it hurt and I skinned my knee," she rambled as her little chin trembled.

"Okay. Let me see." I sat her back down and looked at her ripped jeans. I didn't see any wound through the hole in the knee, so I rolled them up.

Nothing. Just perfect brown skin. "I thought you said you skinned your knee?" I looked up to see her exchanging a guilty glance with Kai.

"Oh, um, I guess I, uh, just thought I skinned it."

"What happened to Kai? He looks like he got the brunt of the fight."

He shook his head miserably. "No. I'm fine," he said quietly.

"You should see Tyler," said Megan. "Kai beat him up for pushing me."

Well, what was I supposed to say to that? I, of course, didn't condone fighting, but the kid had stood up for Megan.

"Mrs. Ruiz?" the principal called to me from the doorway of her office, gesturing for me to join her inside.

"Okay, wait here, Megan. Kai, did they call your dad?"

He nodded. "My nanny is on her way." Of course. The nanny. I was beginning to wonder if he really had a father.

"Thank you for getting here so quickly. Please have a seat," the principal, Ms. Perez, offered. "First of all, please understand that Megan is not in trouble. We needed to ask her some questions about the fight she was involved in and felt it was appropriate to inform a parent about what was going on. She's pretty upset and I think it would be best if you took her home after I talk to her."

"I agree. So, you haven't talked to her, yet?"

She shook her head. "No. You and her brother are listed as guardians on Megan's information card, is that right? I didn't see a parent listed."

"Megan lives with us. Her father does not have guardianship. Were you able to reach Kai's father? He said his nanny was on her way." I was concerned that the boy's father had yet to make an appearance.

"I spoke to him, but he's out of town, so the nanny is the best we can do today." She looked past me to the door and stood to open her office door. I was shocked to see two school police officers entering. Did an elementary school playground fight really merit police involvement?

"Ms. Perez, what's going on here? I thought you said Megan wasn't in trouble?" I asked.

"She's not, but Kai may be. The other boy, Tyler, had to be taken to the hospital."

Holy crap! What had Kai done? He was so small! Was he really capable of putting someone in the hospital?

Ms. Perez called Megan in for questioning; she looked terrified to see the police officers and I saw her eyes start to tear up.

I pulled out the chair next to me and held her hand. "It's okay, Meg. I'm here." She tried to smile, but it didn't quite work.

"All right, Megan." Ms. Perez sat down and opened her notebook. "We just need to hear what happened. Why don't you start from the beginning? Tell us what you were doing at recess."

Megan looked up at me and I nodded in encouragement. "Kai and Mikayla and me were playing by the slide. Tyler and his friends came over and started making fun of us again."

"What did they say?" Ms. Perez asked. Megan

shook her head. "Megan, we need to know what they said. Don't worry. You won't get in trouble for telling us."

"It's really bad," she whispered, looking up at me with her big brown eyes.

My heart about broke in half. "Go ahead, sweetie. You can do this."

She took a deep breath and launched into her story. "Tyler said 'Look at the freak! Let's hear that stupid voice, Stone! I heard they kicked you out of England 'cause you can't talk right!' So, I told him to shut up and go away." Of course she did. She always stood up for the underdog. "Then he pushed me down, hard, and kicked me. Kai got really mad and pushed him back. He knocked Kai down and punched him in the face and said, 'Hey, Stone, bet you don't even have the stones to screw your little girlfriend! But I don't know who'd want to fuck a little Spic like her, anyway.' Then Kai pushed him and Tyler hit his head."

God, what a foul little bully! I hated that my sweet little Megan had to hear something like that, but I knew elementary school kids could be brutal. I squeezed her hand and smiled crookedly at her.

Ms. Perez nodded and continued writing. "Megan, did Kai stand up when he pushed Tyler the second time? Some of the other children said he was still on the ground when Tyler hit his head."

Megan bit her lip and shrugged. "I don't remember."

"Thank you, Megan. Will you wait out in the other room?" She waited until Megan had left and closed the door. "Mrs. Ruiz, according to multiple witnesses, Tyler literally flew across the playground and smashed into the swing set. He was taken away in an ambulance, unconscious, and they think he may have a concussion. The other witnesses all say that Kai didn't get off the ground until *after* Tyler hit his head."

"Who do they say pushed him? They aren't saying it was Megan, are they?" I asked, appalled.

"No, no. No one is saying that," she rushed to assure me. "That's the problem. No one is saying anything. They're making it sound like Tyler just flew across the playground by himself, as if by magic or something."

That caught my attention. I was intimately familiar with what it took to make someone fly across a room or a playground, but how on earth could a child do it? Who was Kai? What was Kai? "Well, that's impossible, of course," I said. "What do you think happened?"

"I really have no idea, Mrs. Ruiz. I need you to speak to Megan tonight and see if she will talk more candidly to you in private. Please call me tomorrow if she tells you anything else." She stood up and handed me a business card with her phone number on it.

As I was walking out, Kai's nanny was walking in. She was a young woman, maybe 25, with an English accent. "Kai Stone! What have you done?" She grabbed him by the arm roughly and pulled him from his seat.

"Hey! Let's dial it down, okay?" I rushed over to her.

She turned to me, fury apparent in her face for a

split second before she visibly changed her approach and body language, letting go of Kai's arm. "Of course," she said in a much calmer voice. "I was just surprised and upset. Kai has a history of, um, fighting in school. I had hoped he was past it, that this would be a new start for him. Apparently not." She spared him an angry glance.

"Miss Landry, we're ready for you and Kai now." Ms. Perez waited by her office door.

Megan stood up and walked over to Kai. She hugged him, whispering something in his ear before letting him go. They apparently had quite a few secrets. Hmmm.

"Kai," I said as he prepared to follow his nanny into the principal's office. He stopped and looked up at me, apprehension written all over his serious little face. "Thank you for defending Megan. It means a lot to me." He smiled very slightly and walked away, following his nanny.

***

"He said what?" Jack was furious, pacing back and forth in our bedroom, running his hands violently through his hair. "I'm gonna kick his ass! Nobody talks about my sister like that!"

"I know, hon. Calm down," I soothed. "The kid is in the hospital with a concussion, so I think you're going to have to wait to kick his ass. And you're going to have to get in line." I was still angry about the whole incident and worried about what effect it would have on Megan.

"Is Megan all right? Is she upset?" he asked.

"I think she's fine. I need to talk to her some more. I'm not sure she understood everything that horrible kid said."

"Son of a bitch!" Jack growled. He sat down on the edge of the bed and put his head in his hands.

I sat beside him and rubbed his back. "It'll be okay, Jack. She's a strong kid. She's going to be fine."

He sat up and pulled me close, kissing my hair. "I hope so. Thanks, babe. You did good today. This parenting stuff sure is a kick in the pants, huh?"

I laughed mirthlessly. "Yeah, for sure."

"So, tell me again how Kai put the kid in the hospital. I wouldn't have thought he had it in him. He's so scrawny."

"I don't think he touched him, Jack. Most of the kids who saw it say Kai was still on the ground when Tyler 'flew' across the playground. That was how the principal put it, by the way. Does that sound familiar to you?" I raised my eyebrows at him.

"Holy shit! Is that kid a Seer? How is that possible?"

"I have no idea! I need to talk to Rémy and maybe Kate. I don't know what to think. I've never heard of a little kid being able to do that. I've never heard of anyone except me being able to do that. And that's not all. Megan said she was pushed and she scraped her knee. When I checked, her jeans were torn, but there was no scrape. She told me she must have been wrong, that she didn't scrape it after all, but Jack, I think she was lying."

"What do you mean? What are you saying?" He

looked perplexed.

I let out a sigh. "Nothing. Never mind. I have no idea what I'm saying." I shook my head at the crazy thoughts I was starting to have. "This is all crazy! There's no way that little kid could have made a bigger kid fly across the playground. They must be wrong or exaggerating or something. Let's go talk to Megan. That was some pretty foul stuff she heard and we should make sure she's doing okay."

We found her sitting on the floor of her bedroom, playing listlessly with a Barbie doll. "Meg, are you okay?" Jack asked as we walked into the room.

"Jack!" She threw herself at him; she had been in her room since we returned home and hadn't seen her brother yet.

"Okay, mija. It's okay." He smoothed her hair as she cried. I couldn't keep my tears at bay either, as I realized she was more upset than I had realized. He calmed her down and asked her to tell him everything that had happened. His jaw flexed as she repeated the horrible comments Tyler had made.

"Meg, do you understand what he said? Do you know what those words mean?" I asked hesitantly.

She nodded slowly. "Yeah, mostly. I've heard Jack say it before." Yikes. What happened to the innocence of childhood?

"I'm sorry, Meg. I shouldn't say it. That's not what I mean when I say it," Jack apologized.

I calmly explained to her what horrid Tyler had been implying, realizing that it was better for her to understand than to be kept in the dark.

"That's awful, Ally. Kai's my friend. He's not

my boyfriend. I don't have a boyfriend. I don't want one. Boys are gross. Except Kai."

"Hey," Jack protested, pulling her onto his lap. "What about me? And Mat? Are we gross?"

"No." She giggled and I was glad to see her back to her more normal self. "You and Mat and Rémy aren't gross, either."

"Meg, I need you to be honest now, okay?" I knelt in front of her and looked into her eyes. "I need you to tell me if Kai was still on the ground when Tyler was pushed into the swing set. Was he?"

Her bottom lip trembled as she nodded.

"Did someone else push Tyler?"

She slowly shook her head.

"How did he get across the playground?" I asked.

"Kai," she whispered. "He's special."

Well, crap. That's what I was afraid of.

We fed and bathed her and tucked her in, telling her that we would sort it all out the next day. Of course I didn't even know if that was possible. As I straightened from giving her a kiss, I noticed the drawings tacked to her wall above her bed. I narrowed my eyes as I realized the boy she had drawn was definitely Kai. But I had seen them long before she had met him at school. My heart pounded and I had to sit on the edge of the bed. "Those pictures. That's Kai, isn't it?" She nodded. "Meg, sweetie, how in the world did you draw Kai before you met him?"

"I saw him in my dreams. He visits me when I'm asleep." Yeah, me too. Crap.

Rémy and Mina came over after we were sure she was asleep. "What are we going to do about the boy?" he asked.

"What can we do? We don't know anything about him," I said. I told them about the drawings and the dreams.

"His last name is Stone, you said?" Mina asked.

I nodded. "I think so. That's what his nanny said. Rémy, can you investigate him?"

"I will certainly try," he promised.

"What do we do in the meantime?" asked Jack. "Should we question him? Should we let Megan be friends with him? I'm really torn because the kid stood up for her. A part of me admires him and is grateful. But another part of me is worried about letting them be friends. I mean, what the hell is he?"

"I don't think we should overreact," I said. Everyone looked at me in surprise. "Listen, Megan and Kai are really close. You didn't see the way she hugged him before we left. I think we need to trust her judgment, at least for now. Trying to keep them apart could backfire. Plus, how in the world do we go about keeping him out of her dreams? Why don't we just keep an eye on them? If we keep them apart, we won't be able to keep a watch on him."

"Should we question him?" Jack asked again.

"Let me try to find out something before we do anything else," Rémy advised. "Let the children be for now."

Chapter Nine

"A man, though wise, should never be ashamed of learning more, and must unbend his mind."
—*Sophocles, Antigone*

Because there was no evidence that he had touched Tyler beyond pushing him the first time, Kai was allowed to return to school the next day. I called Ms. Perez and told her Megan swore Kai was on the ground and did not push the other boy into the swing set; she had no idea how Tyler had hit his head. Ms. Perez had called Tyler's mother and found out that he had a mild concussion and would be returning to school in a few days. He would be attending anti-bullying classes with the school counselor when he returned, as well. That wasn't good enough for Jack and he started giving Megan what he swore were only self-defense lessons.

"She needs to know how to protect herself, querida," he argued. "That's all I'm going to teach her, I promise. The next time someone tries to push her around, she'll be prepared."

"You know she'll be suspended if she punches anyone, don't you? Even if it's in self-defense."

"I'll pick her up from school myself—proudly," he said. "I'll teach you too. Come on, it'll be fun. You need to know how to punch someone without breaking your hand." He kissed my knuckles as he said this last bit. "Next time you hit Rémy, for example."

I smiled reluctantly and pulled him close for a kiss. "I didn't break my hand. I just split it open. And I have no plans to punch him again."

"A guy can hope, can't he?"

I picked Kai and Megan up after school, not even questioning the boy's presence. "Hey guys, how was school? Kai, your eye looks so much better. Wow. I thought it would be swollen shut today."

"He didn't hit me that hard," Kai said quietly. "My nanny put some stuff on it. It's okay."

In the rearview mirror I saw the two children exchange a swift glance. I thought back to Megan's torn jeans and the crazy thoughts I'd had. She had said he was 'special,' but how special?

After snack time, the two disappeared into Megan's room and I could hear her giggles while I started getting dinner ready. As I walked past her bedroom door, left partly open as I had requested, I stopped to peek inside. The children were seated on the floor with a board game between them.

"It was Professor Plum, in the library, with the candlestick," Kai claimed.

Megan placed the cards in the center of the board with a groan. "How do you do that? You are so good at this game!" She flopped backward onto the floor.

Kai laughed, a rusty sound, as if he hadn't used it in a while. My heart went out to him while at the same time I thought I might have a pretty decent idea why he was so good at the game. I left the two of them to their game and went to change into my comfy yoga pants and a sweatshirt.

"Mmm. That smells great," Jack said when he came in about an hour later. He set his backpack on the table and put his arms around me from behind. "But this smells even better." He moved my hair to the side and nuzzled my neck.

I gave the marinara sauce a final stir and turned in his arms. "Hey, you." I reached up on tip-toe to kiss him hello.

"Hey back," he murmured against my lips. "Come here." He picked me up and set me on the counter, pushing my knees open to step between them. "Do you have any idea how many fantasies I have that involve you and this counter?"

I laughed and pulled his face closer. "Well, we have played out a few of those."

"Oh, there are more where those came from. I would be happy to tell you all about them, if you like."

"Definitely, but later. Right now I need a really good kiss."

"A really good one, huh?" He smiled. "Let me see what I can do." Then we both stopped talking. I melted into his kiss, deepening it and sinking my fingers into his thick hair. His hands found their way under my sweatshirt, smoothing over my stomach and creeping up. It was so nice to be able to kiss and not worry about trying not to go too far, as had been a constant challenge during the years we dated. Now nothing was off limits; indeed our only limitation was time and the presence of a child in the house.

"Ugh! They *always* kiss!" said that child from the kitchen doorway. "Gross."

Jack pulled back, smiling grimly as he removed his hand from the very interesting place it had found. "Do I need to remind you that Ally and I are married, brat? Married people like to kiss." He turned and swooped her into his arms, held her upside down, and started tickling her.

"I'm not a brat!"

"Yes, you are. Admit it!"

She giggled wildly while her face turned dark red as the blood rushed to her head. "Okay, okay! I'm a brat!"

I happened to catch a glimpse of Kai's face when I took my eyes off the laughing siblings. There was such intense longing in his eyes that I gasped softly. He tore his gaze away from Jack and Megan and looked at me, quickly schooling his features back to normal.

"Can Kai stay for dinner?" Megan asked as Jack turned her right side up and set her on the floor. "It smells so good, Ally! We're starving!" She turned to Kai and said in a loud stage whisper, "She's not a very good cook yet, but her spaghetti sauce is okay."

Ouch. True, but, still! "Of course he can stay, if he gets permission."

Before they ran off, Jack caught her and

whispered something in her ear. She turned back and ran across the kitchen to hug me. "I'm sorry, Ally. You're a good cook. I didn't mean it."

I hugged her back, meeting Jack's eyes over her head. He winked at me. "That's okay, Meg. I know my cooking sucks most of the time." I kissed the top of her head and sent her off to play until dinner. I turned to Jack. "Thanks for standing up for me, hon, but she's right."

"No, she's not. You're a fine cook." He pulled me back into his arms.

"You are sweet, but a liar. Don't worry. I don't have a lot of pride wrapped up in my cooking skills."

"Well, you have skills in other areas, querida. Let me tell you about a few of my favorites." He whispered some very naughty things in my ear. "You do still need some work on that last one, however. It's a good thing I'm so willing to offer myself for practice."

"You're *so* selfless, Jack."

"I know."

It was interesting to watch Kai eat; he used his knife and fork so differently than the rest of us. He cut his spaghetti into pieces and used his knife to push it on the back of his fork before putting it in his mouth. He stopped chewing when he noticed Megan and me staring.

"Did I do something wrong?" he asked.

"No, no! Of course, not. I'm sorry, Kai. You have impeccable table manners, unlike the rest of us. So, where in England are you from?" I raised my eyebrows at Megan to get her to stop staring.

"London."

"Oh," I said. "When did you move to the U.S.?"

"This summer."

Apparently, one and two word answers were all I was going to get. But I was nothing if not persistent. "So, why did your family move here?" A why question would require at least a couple words.

"My father got a job here." I could almost hear him sigh as he realized I would keep asking. "He works for Intel."

"Do you like it here so far?"

He shrugged. "It's okay, I guess."

I gave up. "So, what was school like today, Meg? Was it fun?"

She had none of Kai's reservations and entertained us for the duration of the meal with a play-by-play of her day at school. It was her job to clear the table and rinse off the plates before putting them in the dishwasher, but Kai manfully volunteered to help. Jack and I retreated to the den for a precious few minutes of peace and quiet.

I was finishing up in the kitchen later that evening while Megan got her bath. She was good at loading the dishwasher, but I always followed up with a general wipe down of the counters and stovetop. As I rinsed the dishcloth, I noticed the small ceramic cat figurine, the one that reminded me of Wicky, was missing from the kitchen windowsill. When I asked Jack about it, he said he hadn't moved it. I asked Megan about it when I tucked her in.

"I don't know where it is, Ally." But I noticed she didn't quite meet my eyes.

"If you broke it or something, Megan, just tell me. It's okay. I won't be mad."

"No." Now she met my eyes. "I didn't break it. I promise."

Hmmm. She wasn't lying about breaking it, but she knew where it was. I decided to let it rest, for now.

***

"Ms. Ruiz? Can I talk to you about something?" It was one of the boys from the third period English 12 class. "It's about the lesson you did today."

"Um, sure." Crap! What was his name? Kevin? Kyle? "What did you need?" I hoped it wouldn't take too long since I was on my way out and Jack was picking me up. He had driven my SUV so he could get new tires.

"I could walk out with you," he offered. "You want me to carry anything for you?"

The way he said it, with a hopeful puppy look on his face, made me realize I needed to nip this in the bud. Sheesh! "No, thanks. I've got it." I headed out the classroom door, intent on making record time to the staff parking lot. The kid—what's his name— was obviously one of the popular, athletic type guys, and was acting a bit too flirty for my comfort level. "So, what do you need?" I asked again, trying to sound as professional as possible.

"Oh, yeah. So I was thinking about that story, the one we read today, the um, one by Faulkner."

"*A Rose for Emily*? What about it? Did you like it?" I tried to keep the patent disbelief from my voice.

"Yeah, it was great. I was hoping we could talk more about the interpretation?"

Okay, sure. Whatever. I indulged him and we discussed the various interpretations, including Faulkner's own, while he walked me to the parking lot. When we reached the edge of the lot, I stopped and turned to him. "You don't need to walk me all the way to my car."

"No, it's okay. I think I should." He looked over my shoulder. "I don't like the looks of that guy over there. I better walk you to your car."

I turned to see whom he was talking about and smiled as I turned back. "I'll be fine. That's my husband, and that's my car."

"Oh. You're married. Great." He sounded less than thrilled. "Well, see you tomorrow."

I approached Jack as he leaned against the front of the SUV, hands in his jeans pockets, wearing his black leather jacket and looking every inch the bad boy I had thought he was in high school. I saw he wasn't looking at me so much as he was watching something behind me, eyes narrowed, a rather dangerous look on his face. "Hey, you," I said.

"Hey back," he said as he pulled me into his arms and lowered his head to kiss me. I was expecting a more perfunctory greeting than what I got. He opened his mouth over mine, his tongue invading, stroking mine.

"Mmmm. Jack!" I yelped and pulled back when I felt his hands curve around my bottom. "What the hell? This is where I work!"

"Sorry." He had the grace to look somewhat

shame-faced. "Just sending a message."

I turned to look; Kevin/Kyle was walking away dejectedly. "Oh, Jack! You can't think—eww! He's one of my students!"

"Yeah, well you didn't have to watch him looking at your ass as you walked away."

"Really? That's disgusting."

"No, it's not. He's a perfectly normal, red-blooded American boy and it's an ass worth looking at. I just let him know you're taken. You're mine."

"Ooh, that sounds so possessive. Are you sure you can handle me?" I challenged, irritated at his possessiveness.

"That's what I was doing."

"Oh, yeah?"

"Yeah."

We stared at each other, arms crossed, eyebrows raised, daring the other to continue.

"I'm sorry," he said finally. "I shouldn't have said it like that. Forgive me?"

I smiled. "Of course. I am yours, but you should let me say it. It comes off a bit Neanderthal when you say it."

He laughed and pulled me back into his arms. "Okay. I'll let you say it from now on. For what it's worth, you can say that I'm yours, and that I'm taken—anytime you want."

"I will keep that in mind. Now, don't we need to go pick up Megan and take her to Trina's? I was promised a date tonight. All this talk of possessiveness has put me in a mood."

"A mood, huh? Tell me more. What kind of mood?" he asked while nibbling on my neck.

"Mmmm, yeah. A frisky mood." I was losing my power to concentrate.

"Frisky, huh? That does sound promising." He pushed me into the car and kissed me fiercely before climbing in the driver's side and putting the key into the ignition. He let it idle for a moment while he sat gripping the steering wheel. "Aw, screw it," he said before hauling me into his lap.

I had several buttons undone when my ringing cell phone saved us from a truly terrible heat-of-the-moment decision that the dark tinted windows might not have concealed. "Hello." I crawled back to my seat, pushing my hair out of my face and trying vainly to button my shirt with one hand. Jack was banging his head lightly against the steering wheel.

"Ally, love, it's Grams."

"Hey, Grams. Um, how are you?"

"I'm fine, dear. I need you and Jack to come for dinner tonight. Can Trina watch Megan? I need to talk to you both." She sounded unusually flustered.

"Grams, how about tomorrow night? We already have plans tonight." I winced as I said it, hating to refuse my grandmother, who asked so little of me. But Jack and I *needed* time alone together.

"Is there any way you could reschedule, dear? I really need you to come tonight. Fionnuala is here. She called from the airport about an hour ago, and well, she's here. She needs to talk to you. Rather urgently, in fact."

Well, shit. I had some rather urgent needs of my own at the moment. "Okay. Sure, Grams. Of course. We'll be there in about an hour." I hung up and sat back with a groan.

"Are you kidding me?" Jack asked with a sigh.

"I'm so sorry, hon."

"No, it's not your fault, querida. Well, let's get this done. For the record, I had a legit date planned tonight."

I smiled and crawled back to give him a lingering kiss. "I believe you. Raincheck?"

"You are killing me." He surprised me by pulling me back suddenly for another hard, quick kiss. "We'll get back to this discussion later."

Grams had ordered takeout, a testament to her flustered state: she would normally never invite guests over for takeout.

"Ah, Ally, dear. Sure, it's good to see you." Fionnuala smothered me in a hug.

"Hey, Fionnuala," I choked out. "Great to see you too. You remember Jack, don't you?"

"Of course. Jack, my dear, how are you?" She practically pushed me away to grab him for a hug. "So, you two sneaked away and got married in Paris, did you? And my darling Mina married that French boy!"

"His name is Rémy, and they'll be here any minute," I said, exasperated. They arrived within minutes and we all sat down for the impromptu dinner party.

"Fionnuala, why didn't you let us know you were coming?" I asked. "We would have loved to have you stay with us." I saw Jack try to hide his panicked look.

"Well, my dear, Mina's husband isn't the only one who has been investigating Luc Séverin."

"Fionnuala! My husband has a name," Mina scolded.

"Well, I'm sure I'm sorry," Fionnuala exclaimed. "Maybe if he hadn't whisked you away without so much as a 'by your leave,' I would remember his name." She sniffed, her displeasure apparent.

I saw Rémy take Mina's hand and shake his head slightly, an amused look on his face. Mina rolled her eyes.

"So, what did you discover?" I asked impatiently.

"We have good reason to believe Luc is here in the United States. I thought you should know."

I gulped. Great. If he was in the U.S., he could easily be in Albuquerque. Why wouldn't he be, after all? The one thing he wanted was to control me. We had hoped to escape by staging a fake ascension, but had apparently only bought ourselves some time.

We spent the rest of the meal discussing what this could possibly mean and what, if anything, we could do about it. I lost my appetite the second Luc was mentioned, but pushed the food around on my plate in an attempt to fool my grandmother and husband. As I listened to the others hash and re-hash the situation, I found myself moving through an array of emotions: numb disbelief was first, then fear, and finally anger; burning, searing fury that churned the acid in my stomach. I was seriously pissed off. I was so completely *done* with this whole situation!

I could tell when Rémy picked up on my mood and thoughts. "Well, we can't solve anything tonight," he said. "I suggest we all go home and carry on as normal until we know more."

Jack took my hand as we walked to our car. "You okay, babe? What can I do? It's still early. Do you want to go see a movie or something? We could go grab something to eat afterward, since you didn't eat much." So he had noticed. He always noticed.

"You know what I want?"

"Anything. Name it," he promised.

We reached the SUV and I backed him against the driver's door, stepped as close as I possibly could and pulled his face down to mine. "What I want more than anything else is to go home and finish what we started earlier. Please, Jack. I don't want to think about Luc anymore tonight. Please."

"Of course." He kissed me. "Let's go."

***

The heavenly fragrance of coffee woke me the following morning. Since Jack's arm was still draped over me, I knew Rémy must be here.

"Why haven't we changed the locks?" Jack grumbled against my hair.

"I have no idea." I kissed him softly and sat up. "Go back to sleep. I'll get rid of him." I found some yoga pants and a t-shirt and padded into the kitchen where I poured myself a cup of the delicious coffee he always managed to produce.

"Good morning, cherié." He looked up from his iPad. "Late night?"

I shrugged. "Not really. We got home pretty early."

"Well, since I followed a trail of discarded clothing from the front door, I just assumed…" He let his statement trail off suggestively.

"Shut up, Rémy," I said without much rancor, although I could feel the heat rising in my cheeks. "What do you want? I assume there is a valid reason for your presence?"

"I came to invite you and Jack for breakfast. Mina is making French toast and I think we all need to discuss Fionnuala's news."

Jack appeared in the kitchen, wearing jeans but no shirt. I handed him a cup of coffee before I sat down across from Rémy. "Are you up for breakfast with Mina and Rémy, hon?"

"Hmmm." He sipped his coffee and cleared his throat. "Sure, if you want. Are we talking about Luc?"

I nodded. "Yeah. It's probably a good idea."

"Okay," said Jack. "On one condition: we eat first and then talk. I know you won't be able to eat if we try to talk about Luc during breakfast."

"Deal." I smiled.

We let ourselves into their kitchen fifteen minutes later. Mina was turning pieces of bread in a skillet while Rémy sliced fruit into a bowl.

"Come in. There's fresh orange juice on the table." He placed the fruit bowl between us and crossed to the stove, where he put his arms around Mina from behind and nuzzled her neck, making her giggle. He started whispering naughty things to her in French and I could see her blush from where I sat.

I rolled my eyes at Jack. "Can we get on with

this?"

"But of course, cherié," Rémy said, laughing. He took the platter of French toast from Mina and set it on the table. "Bon appetit."

Jack watched me like a hawk while we ate and insisted we only discuss mundane, pleasant things until the plates were cleared. I still wasn't hungry, but I loved him, so I ate as much from my plate as I possibly could.

"Now," said Mina as Rémy cleared the table. "Let's see if we can figure out what to do."

"Is there any way to figure out where he is?" Jack asked. "Rémy, can you track him down?"

"I have been trying all night. He arrived in New York in July, but has since disappeared. I fear he may be using another name."

"Shit," Jack muttered. "We can't catch a break."

"On the contrary," said Rémy. "This is our break. He is here, in Albuquerque. I'm certain of it. This will be over soon. We are close to the end game. He will make his move in the very near future."

"But what do we do in the meantime?" I asked.

"We prepare," Mina stated grimly.

"Great," I said. "What does that mean?"

What it meant was every extra minute of my day was now spent at Mina and Rémy's house, practicing my defensive powers and perfecting our mental communication with each other. We were still attempting to keep the whole psychic thing from Megan, but my excuses for constantly escaping across the street were starting to wear thin by the second week. Jack was a trooper, taking over all the dinner and dish chores, which was actually better for everyone's digestion. Kai was a frequent dinner guest, but always refused our offers of a ride home afterward.

"Ally, can you help me with my English homework after dinner?" Megan asked one evening while we ate the tacos Jack had prepared, black bean for me, beef for everyone else. Kai had stared at them dubiously for a moment, but with Megan's encouragement, seemed to be enjoying his dinner.

"Meg, she has to go to Rémy's after dinner. You know that," Jack admonished quietly.

"No." I shook my head and reached for more Spanish rice, for which Jack had a real flair. "You know what? I can help you with your homework, sweetie. I don't need to rush off right after dinner every single night. Rémy and Mina can wait for a while."

At Kai's questioning look, Megan filled him in. "Ally is doing a special project with them. She says it's a surprise and she can't tell me what it is yet."

"Kai, is this the first time you've tried Mexican food?" I tried to get Megan off the subject of my nightly disappearances.

He nodded. "It's good. Thank you." He was nothing if not polite.

"Just wait 'til you taste my Auntie Trina's enchiladas, Kai! They're amazing! And my Aunt Gloria makes the best menudo in the whole world. You can come with us to our next family party," Megan said, oblivious to the faintly panicked look on Kai's face.

"What's menudo?" he asked.

"A truly disgusting soup made with the lining of a cow's stomach," I said.

"Are you having me on?" he asked, sounding very British.

Megan giggled. "No, she's telling the truth, except it's delicious. Ally doesn't eat meat, so she doesn't know what's good. Besides, you told me all about blood pudding! That's gross!"

I had seen Mina and the other Irish Seers eat this atrocity and completely agreed with Megan, but there was no need to be rude to a guest. "Meg, let's not insult someone's food choices."

"That's rich." Jack laughed. "This from the woman who refused to kiss me after I ate menudo. Seems a little unfair, huh, Kai?"

The boy smiled and nodded slightly. "I'll try the menudo if you promise to try blood pudding someday, Megan."

She scrunched up her nose, but stuck out her hand. "Deal." They both shook on it.

Megan and Kai cleared the table while Jack and I spent a few minutes talking quietly in our bedroom. The new practice schedule was seriously cutting into our alone time. Kai left to walk home while Megan got her homework out and set it up on the dining room table so I could help her. We were wrapping up an essay she had to write about a book she had read in class while Jack was cleaning up the kitchen.

"Meg, where did you put the salt shaker?" he asked as he joined us at the table.

"On the stove, with the pepper."

"It's not there," he said. She shrugged and I met

Jack's confused gaze. This would be the second missing item in the last week.

"You're late," Rémy said when I let myself into their house a half hour later.

"Sorry," I said huffily. "I needed to help Meg with her homework. I have a family, you know!"

"I know that, but we have much to do and no idea of how much time we have left. We can't afford to get lazy."

"You're calling me lazy?"

"All right, you two! Cool it!" Mina came in with tea. "Settle down. Let's not let the stress get to us, okay?" She placed her hands on our shoulders and I felt her soothing calm flow into me.

"You're like the People Whisperer, Mina. Maybe you could get your own cable show," I said. I reached up and touched her hand. "Thanks."

"*Je regret, mon ange*," Rémy pulled her onto his lap and kissed her. "Sorry, cherié," he said to me.

"Did you tell her?" Mina asked.

"Tell me what?"

"Grandmére called today. She and my grandfather will be here this weekend for a short visit." At my questioning look he continued. "Apparently, she has had another prophecy, one she feels is important enough to justify a trip over here."

"Great." I dropped my head onto my arms. "There goes my weekend too. If I don't get a date night with my husband soon, it's not going to be pretty!"

Mina reached across and patted my hand sympathetically. "I know, Ally. This will all be over soon. I really feel it. So does Rémy."

"So, what's this new prophecy?" I asked, looking up.

Rémy shrugged. "She wouldn't say. She says she won't tell anyone except Grandpére until she gets here. I have a feeling this prophecy will be 'revealed' by our new Oracle."

"Fabulous," I groused. "Just what I need."

***

Jack and I decided to host dinner for Kate and Phillipe Saturday night. We were making pasta—something I could usually manage without a complete disaster—and Tara had volunteered to take Megan off our hands for a few hours so we could talk without having to watch our words. Megan had somehow wrangled an invitation for Kai as well, and it turned into a movie and pizza outing. Jack was putting the finishing touches on the sauce while I chopped vegetables for a salad when Rémy and Mina arrived with our weekend guests.

"It smells divine in here!" Phillipe exclaimed as he pulled me in for a hug. "Ally, you look wonderful. Marriage certainly suits you. Jack, it is good to see you again." They shook hands while Kate commandeered me for a hug.

Rémy had brought wine, which he poured and handed around. He offered a toast and we all partook of the crackers and cheese I had set out. "So, Grandmére, let us hear the prophecy, please."

"Wouldn't you all rather wait until after dinner?" she asked.

"It would be better to get it over with," I said.

"Tara is supposed to keep Megan busy for a few more hours, but you never can tell with kids."

"Ah, yes." Phillipe smiled. "I look forward to meeting Jack's little sister. I have heard so much about her over the years."

"Yeah, well she doesn't know anything about all the Seer stuff, so we should get that out of the way well before she's due back. Plus, she has a friend with her, and we sure don't want to talk in front of him. Actually, the friend needs to be a topic of our discussion," I added. At Kate's raised eyebrows, I shook my head. "Later, okay?"

Kate nodded. "Fine. Well, let's get this over with. This is the prophecy I received four days ago. I've told no one, except Phillipe." She set her wine down, closed her eyes, took a moment of silence, as if she was gathering her thoughts and then intoned,

"Light and dark will battle for preeminence. An ancient evil will return. Darkness shrouds the origins. Blood will be the price."

She sat down and took a sip of wine.

We all sat quietly for a full two minutes before Rémy broke the silence. "Well, that certainly sounds cheerful. Do you have any idea what it means, Grandmére?"

"None. But—" she began, but broke off and sipped her wine again.

"What is it, Kate?" I asked.

"Nothing. It's just that this prophecy was different somehow. Never mind. I'm sure it's nothing. The important thing is to have the new

Oracle receive this newest prophecy and release it to the Conseil and the Council very soon."

"Yeah, yeah," I muttered. "Would it possible for us to eat dinner first? I don't think I could possibly prophesy on an empty stomach." That earned me a few chuckles and Jack and I retreated to the kitchen to bring the food.

We put aside thoughts and discussion of the dark prophecy and enjoyed our meal while we caught up. Kate informed us Geneviève was beginning to show and Arnaud continued to spoil her dreadfully. They were looking for a house close to Rouen so he could be close to work, where they could settle down and raise their family. It sounded so nice and I couldn't completely restrain an envious sigh. Jack noticed and reached over to squeeze my hand briefly. I wanted to forget all about Seers and prophecies and be able to concentrate on my husband and the family we were building.

Megan and Kai returned in time for dessert, an exhausted-looking Tara following behind. "They both ate their weight in pepperoni pizza, so I don't know how they'll stuff in any dessert—" She broke off when she entered the dining room and noticed everyone staring at Kate and Kai, who were standing across from each other.

"You?" Kate asked, choking.

"You," whispered Kai.

"What the hell?" muttered Jack.

Kai recovered first. "I've seen you in my dreams. You speak in riddles."

"I've seen you, as well, but not in my dreams. And you were older. But it was definitely you,"

Kate said, coming close to Kai, reaching out her hand to touch him. It didn't surprise me when he backed away.

"I have to go," he said. "My father will be angry if I'm late."

"Kai, wait!" Megan followed him to the front door.

He stopped and turned to her as he opened the door. "Bye, Megan. See you later. Sorry."

"Kate, what was that all about?" I asked, crossing to her and taking her hand. She sat, pale and worried. Jack hurried to the kitchen and returned with a glass of water for her, placing it in her hand and making sure she drank before answering me.

"You remember I mentioned this prophecy was different? Well, when I had the prophecy, I saw that boy clearly, only he was a few years older. But it was him. I know that for a fact."

I believed her; after all, I had seen the same thing during my last nightmare/vision.

Megan returned to the room, so we all awkwardly stopped talking. "That was weird. What did you mean? Why did Kai run away?" she asked Kate.

Kate looked to Jack and me for permission. He looked at me, searching, and I nodded briefly; it seemed the time had come to let Megan in on our little secret. Kate gestured for Meg to sit down and proceeded to tell her about the wonderful world of Seers.

"Wait. So, all of you are Seers? You're all psychic?" She looked around the room.

"Except for Jack and me," said Tara. "We're mere humans."

"God, Tara! We're all human. You're going to make her think we're freaks or something," I complained.

Megan, who had a deep vein of sweetness running through her, got up and crossed to where I was sitting, and leaned against me. "I would never think that, Ally. You're my sister."

"Thanks, Meg. I'm so glad we're sisters now." I hugged her to my side.

"So, will you read my mind?" she asked. "Please?"

I laughed slightly. "Well, I could try, but Rémy is so much better at it than me."

"Come here, Megan," Rémy commanded as he held his hand out toward her. She hesitated, suddenly shy around him, but he smiled and she put her hand in his. He pulled her onto his lap and kissed her hair. "Hmm, let's see now. This is very interesting! You are thinking about how much fun it is to finally have a sister and you are so glad to live with Jack and Ally. Also, you are worried that Kai is mad at you and won't want to be your friend anymore. I can tell you that is ridiculous. He's lucky to have you for a friend. And most importantly, you're hoping that Ally will let you have dessert, even though you ate too much pizza. I think your chances are pretty good for that last one." Before she hopped off his lap, he leaned forward to whisper in her ear. She stopped to look in his eyes, a serious expression on her face. He smiled slightly and nodded. She hugged him and then hopped down.

What was that last part about? I asked him mentally as Megan pulled me toward the kitchen for her dessert.

She's feeling very ordinary and not special right now. She knows Kai is special, but is afraid to ask about him. I assured her that she is, indeed, very special, and that we will not drive Kai away. She feels very strongly about him, cherié. We must tread lightly there.

We took a break from shoptalk while we had dessert. I had bought a berry and cream layer cake rather than attempt to make anything on my own. I do know my limitations. While Jack tucked Megan in, I took the opportunity to quiz Kate about Kai.

"Is he a Seer? Can you tell anything without touching him?"

"Most definitely, which is unusual. He is a Seer, but there is more. I don't know what else he is, but I am afraid for him." She shivered as she said it.

My stomach cramped as she spoke. I didn't know who or what Kai Stone was, but he had staunchly defended Megan from a bully and had earned my gratitude. I also saw in him a lonely boy with an absentee father and a negligent nanny who needed the kind of love a real family could provide.

"I haven't had a chance to tell you, but I finally got a report back from the private detective I hired to look into the boy's background," Rémy said as he poured more wine for everyone. "There is no record of a Kai Stone being born in London or the surrounding area ten years ago. I had them check a year in either direction with the same results. They will continue to check into birth records in other parts of the country, but I have a feeling the result will be the same."

"What does this mean?" I asked, looking around at the faces staring back at me.

"That boy is not who he says he is," Mina said.

Part Three: Oracle

Chapter Ten

"Good advice, if there's any good in suffering.
Quickest is best when trouble blocks the way."
—Sophocles, *Antigone*

Kate and Phillipe stayed through the weekend and insisted I spend quite a bit of time with them, preparing for my first big prophecy as the Oracle. I had a three-day fall break coming up at the end of the following week, so we had decided it was a perfect opportunity to make a quick trip to France to establish myself more firmly as the Oracle. We planned to tell them that I had had the new prophecy at home and had decided it was too important to talk about over the phone. Rémy made the travel arrangements and Jack made arrangements for Trina and Manny to keep Megan for a few days. I insisted he go with us; I was planning to make sure the Conseil understood we were a package deal from now on. Kate felt that my willingness to travel to France a few times per year would soften them about my sudden disappearance this past summer.

Megan's fears that Kai wouldn't want to be her friend were unfounded and they were thick as thieves again but at school only; Kai hadn't come home with her after school since the night he had met Kate. Rémy and I had multiple conversations about how to deal with this new development but finally decided to let it go for the time being and adopted a wait-and-see attitude. We all seemed to sense he was important, but none of us had any clue as to how or why and were afraid of scaring him away.

Megan was seated at the kitchen table, working on math problems while I chopped vegetables for a big pot of homemade soup I was hoping would be edible. The recipe seemed simple, but I had failed epically at simpler recipes. I still needed to spend a few hours with Rémy and Mina later tonight, but for now I was enjoying some domestic time.

I was chopping a carrot, trying to make even-sized pieces, when the voice started in my head.

"Ally. Ally! Listen to me, please! I don't have much time. I have to warn you."

I vaguely remember setting down the knife so I wouldn't slice off a finger and leaning my arms against the counter. I closed my eyes and was swept into a vision.

"Ally, follow me. Hurry!" The boy, the older version of Kai, motioned for me to follow him, his green eyes intense as they stared into mine. We were in a stark, white room of some sort. It

reminded me of the time I had talked to Ashley Hayes when I had been conked on the head by her killer.

"You're Kai, aren't you?"

He turned and nodded. "Hurry, Ally. We don't have much time."

"Where are we going? I don't trust you, Kai. I don't know who or what you are. I can't follow you."

He looked at me sadly. "There's no reason to trust me. I don't know who or what I am, either. All I know is that Megan is in danger. Please, Ally. She's the only thing that's important right now."

"Why? Why is she in danger, Kai? Tell me!" I demanded.

Kai moved to open the door we had reached. "I can't tell you. He won't let me! But you have to save her!" He pushed the door open and we were suddenly in the place of my last vision: the dark, cavernous room with broken bottles and trash littering the brick floor. In places the bricks were torn up, forming piles and impassable rough spots. The square windows of green and brown glass, many of them broken and allowing cold air and moonlight to stream in, reached high toward the scaffolding overhead.

"Where are we? What is this place?"

He didn't answer, but kept leading me farther into the cavernous structure. My heart beat wildly against the waves of danger pressing in on me; I wasn't safe here.

"Kai, we need to get out of here. It's not safe. Please, let's go," I begged.

"We can't. Not yet. Not until we find her. She's here somewhere." He turned to motion me on and I could see his eyes nearly overflowing with tears. He had been crying in the last vision and I realized that this must be just before that time. He led me up several flights of stairs to a platform of some sort.

Something was ahead, maybe fifty feet away. It looked like a pile of discarded clothing from here. Kai gave an exclamation of some sort and began running toward it. He fell to his knees beside the pile and started weeping. I crept closer, the feeling of dread pulsing heavy in the air around me. The pile of discarded clothing resolved itself into Megan, lying crumpled and unconscious at his feet. I reached out to touch his thin, shaking shoulder.

He turned to me, tears streaming from his piercing green eyes. *"I'm sorry, Ally. I didn't want this. She isn't part of this. I tried to save her, but he made me! I'm so sorry!"*

"Kai! What have you done? Is she…?"

"No," he cried as he wiped his eyes. *"She's alive. It's you he wants, Ally. He used her to get to you. You have to protect her! I came to warn you."*

"Ally! What's wrong? Ally! Wake up!" I could hear Megan calling to me, panicked out of her little mind, but it was from a great distance. I couldn't get through to her to tell her not to worry. "Rémy? Are you at home? Oh, God, Rémy! Something's wrong with Ally! She fell on the kitchen floor and she won't wake up! I'm scared, Rémy!" I knew she was talking on my cell phone to him, but I still couldn't open my eyes or speak or even move. "Okay.

Hurry!" I could feel her rubbing my hand between hers. My heart broke as she sobbed.

The kitchen door flew open and Rémy and Mina burst through. I felt myself being lifted and carried through to the living room, where I was placed on the sofa. I felt Mina's cool hands on my face and heard her soft voice urging me to wake up. I heard Rémy on the phone with Jack, urging him to come home *now*. That finally caused me to push through whatever barrier was holding me half in and half out the vision: I had to tell Jack I was okay. I didn't want him rushing home, speeding and possibly getting in a wreck.

"I'm okay. I'm awake." At least that's what I was trying to say. All that came out was a garbled mess of sound.

"Okay, sweetie. It's okay." I heard Mina crooning as she placed a cool cloth on my forehead. By the time Jack burst through the door I was sitting up, sipping a glass of water. I hadn't spoken yet.

"What happened?" he asked as he knelt in front of me, pushing my hair back.

"I'm okay," I whispered; this time I actually said the words. "I'm sorry I scared everyone. Where's Meg?"

She had been standing out of the way, beside the sofa. "I'm here."

I held my hand out to her. "Come here, Meg." I pulled her to sit next to me and cuddled her. "I'm so sorry I scared you. I had a vision. Sometimes I pass out when I have them. I'm so sorry you were scared. I'm fine. I promise."

"Okay." She sniffed.

"Tell us," Rémy commanded.

I shook my head at him. *Not with Megan here. It was about her. And Kai. I don't want to talk about it in front of her.* "I can't right now. I need to rest. Please."

"Okay." Jack, a man of few words, took the water glass out of my hands and scooped me up into his arms. He carried me to our bedroom and laid me gently on our bed. He pulled the afghan up and sat beside me. "Are you okay, Ally? Really?"

I nodded and placed my hand over his. "I really am. It was one of those visions, Jack. The kind that really do a number on me. I scared Megan. I'm so sorry." I felt a tear roll down my cheek.

"Hey." He reached to wipe it away. "She's fine. She's strong. I'll talk to her. You need to rest. We'll talk about the vision later, okay?"

I nodded gratefully. I wasn't sure I'd be able to tell what had happened without breaking down. I needed some time to gather my thoughts. I rolled over and closed my eyes, intending to rest for a few minutes. When I woke, the bedroom was dark and a delicious aroma wafted in from the kitchen. Jack must have finished the soup I had started earlier. The bedside clock said it was nearly nine o'clock. Embarrassed, I shoved my feet in my slippers and headed out to the kitchen.

Mina, Rémy, and Jack were seated around the table, talking in hushed tones. "Ah, cherié. You look much better. You have your color back. You were pale as a ghost when I first got here." Rémy poured a glass of red wine and set it at the empty place, gesturing for me to sit. Mina stood up, saying that she would get me a bowl of soup. Jack stood and pulled me into his arms, tipping my face up, searching.

"How do you feel?"

"I'm better. I can't believe I slept so long."

"Don't worry about it." He leaned down to kiss me softly.

"All right. Enough of that!" Mina scolded gently. "She needs nourishment right now."

I sat and tasted the soup. It was delicious and I ate an entire bowl before stopping to say anything else. I was ravenous! Mina took my empty bowl and refilled it silently. "This is great. It makes me mad that you're a better cook than I am, Jack."

He placed a small dish of crackers beside my plate and leaned down to kiss the top of my head. "Mina made it."

"Thanks, Mina. Where's Meg?"

"I tucked her in a little while ago. She was pretty tired." Jack wouldn't quite meet my eyes.

I pushed my soup away, disgusted at how I must have terrified her. "God. I'm so sorry, Jack."

"Hey." He sat across from me, forcing me to look at him. "She's fine. She's worried about you, but she's fine."

"Tell us about the vision, cherié," Rémy suggested.

I did, leaving nothing out. I told them how it appeared to be a prequel to the previous vision and how I had been able to actually converse with Kai. "He was trying to warn me. He said Megan was being used to get to me. He must have been talking about Luc."

"I agree," said Rémy.

"What are we going to do about it?" I asked, standing up to pace. "I can't stand just sitting around and waiting for something to happen!"

"I have a few ideas, but I need some time to sort them out."

"We don't have time, Rémy!" I felt in my very soul that time was short.

"I know." He sounded so calm and assured. "We will talk when we're in France. We will make plans. I promise this will be over soon."

"We have to keep Megan safe. That's got to be our number one priority."

"It is, cherié. I swear we will do everything we can to keep her safe."

***

I jerked awake, unsure of what had woken me. I couldn't remember a nightmare and had, in fact been sleeping soundly and peacefully. I lay still, trying to figure out what was bothering me. That's when I heard a muffled *clunk* from the kitchen area. My heart started pounding, although I told myself it was only the dog. I lay still and waited. *Thud.*

"Jack!" I nudged him and whispered furiously. "Wake up!"

"Wha? Huh?" he mumbled sleepily.

"I think there's someone in the house."

Clunk.

"Shit!" he said as he threw the covers off. He reached into the closet and retrieved the nine-millimeter handgun he kept in a gun safe. "Stay with Megan," he ordered as he inserted a clip into the gun and headed into the hallway.

Oh God, oh God, oh God, I prayed as I ran across the hall to Megan's bedroom. Her door was cracked and I opened it slowly. She was asleep, lying on her stomach, while Sodapop stood on the end of her bed, growling. He stopped and wagged his tail when he saw me. "Good boy," I whispered and moved across the room to stroke his head. He spared me a lick before jumping off the bed and running out of the room, probably to give Jack backup. I heard his toenails scrabbling on the kitchen tile as I knelt beside Megan's bed, not satisfied until I brushed the hair out of her face and felt her even breathing. She slept like the dead unless she had a nightmare, so I pulled the covers up and tucked them around her shoulders before tip-toeing out and closing the bedroom door behind me. Heart still pounding, I crept as quietly as I could toward the kitchen.

"Jack?" I reached out to touch his back as he stood by the kitchen door, which was open to the backyard.

He jumped and cursed loudly. "Jesus, Ally! You scared the shit out of me! You do know I have gun, don't you? I could have shot you! I told you to stay with Meg!" He ran his free hand through his hair and turned to look at me. "Sorry. I didn't mean to yell."

"It's okay. Meg's still sound asleep. What's Soda doing?" The blue heeler was running around the perimeter of the yard, growling and snuffling.

"Where's the flashlight?" he asked, not

answering my question.

I turned and fished it out of the junk drawer and handed it to him. He turned it on and walked out into the yard after the dog.

"Soda?" he called in a hushed voice. "Get over here, boy!" The dog kept running around the yard, barking and growling. "Goddammit, Soda, get over here!"

"Jack, what's going on?"

He gave up on the dog and jogged over to me. "The back door was open when I came out to the kitchen. I think you should call Brian. Ally? Sweetheart? Hey!" He shook me slightly. "Are you okay?"

I nodded mechanically and went back to the bedroom for my phone to call my stepdad. As I hung up, I heard Rémy in my head.

I'm coming in the front door. Tell Jack not to shoot me, please.

I returned to the kitchen as I heard Rémy's key in the lock. "Rémy's on his way in and he doesn't want you to shoot him." Jack had managed to get the dog back in the kitchen and was examining the lock on the door. Rémy appeared and the two men conferred while I decided to make a pot of coffee to keep my hands busy. My mind was numb; I couldn't seem to wrap it around the concept that someone had broken into our house while we were sleeping. I knew I'd be angry soon, but right now I couldn't feel much of anything.

Within fifteen minutes we had two patrol cars and Brian at our house, inspecting all the doors and windows. Jack, Rémy, and I sat at the kitchen table, mugs of untouched coffee and the nine-millimeter gun between us.

"Please tell me you have a permit for that," said Brian as he poured himself a cup of coffee. Jack simply nodded. "And you keep it locked up, away from your sister?"

"Of course." Jack sighed, sounding beyond exhausted. "I have a gun safe in our bedroom closet."

"Good." Brian leaned against the counter and took a sip of his coffee. "It looks like whoever it was broke into your house through the kitchen door. They picked the lock somehow, but it looks like a pro job. We've dusted for prints, but I'm willing to bet they wore gloves. The only prints we'll find will be yours."

"What did you find in the yard?" Rémy asked. "The dog was going crazy out there."

"A few footprints and trampled bushes. Looks like it was a man, judging by the size of the prints. He apparently vaulted over the back fence. How did you know what was happening?" he asked. "Did Ally call you?"

"Not on the phone," Rémy replied and took a sip of his coffee.

"Never mind. Sorry I asked," muttered Brian. He was well aware of the psychic connection we had, but preferred to pretend it didn't exist.

"Why is this happening?" I whispered. "What did we do?"

Jack lifted his head off his arms and reached for me. "Come here, babe." I gladly moved to sit on his lap, curling into his comforting warmth and burying my face against his neck, inhaling the scent that brought my world back into alignment.

"Call your mom, Ally. Please. I'm sure she's freaking out. She would have been here, but she didn't want to wake Elijah." Brian ruffled my hair before he left the kitchen to join the other policemen.

I called her, assuring her that we were fine and I would see her in the morning. It took a full two hours before Brian and the other officers left, telling us they would file a report, but that was all they could do at this point. Brian made Jack promise to call our alarm service in the morning to upgrade to a system that monitored for nighttime intruders. I thought guiltily that I was pretty sure we already paid for that service, but I had never gotten into the habit of setting the 'at home' alarm at night. I would certainly never neglect to set it again. Rémy went back across the street to Mina and we were finally able to go back to bed, but neither of us felt much like sleeping. I lay in Jack's arms, curled against his warm chest.

"It was Luc, wasn't it?" I asked.

He stroked my hair and I felt him nod. "Probably. I can't imagine it was just a random break-in."

"What does he want, Jack?" I felt the tears slip down my cheeks. "Why won't he leave us alone?"

"I don't know babe. I just don't know."

We were bleary-eyed in the morning, but Megan had somehow slept through the whole drama and bounced out to the kitchen, cheerful and ready for breakfast, chattering about what she and her Auntie

Trina were going to do this weekend.

"She said we could go to the zoo on Saturday and we could have a picnic! I wish Kai could go with us, but he said he's grounded. As soon as he's not grounded, can he come over? Please?"

I met Jack's sleepy gaze across the table and he nodded briefly. We would have a few questions for Kai, or whatever his name really was soon. "Sure, sweetie. It'll be nice to see him again."

***

The days seemed to rush by and before I knew it I was sitting beside Jack, with Mina and Rémy across the aisle from us, on our way to Paris. If I ever found the need to travel economy class again, I was in trouble; my standards had been raised impossibly high. Although I was exhausted from my student teaching schedule and all the preparation for this trip—not to mention the crazy visions and the break-in—I couldn't quiet my mind enough to sleep. Jack didn't seem to have the same problem, judging by the even breathing and occasional soft snore. I smiled ruefully and contented myself with rereading *Antigone* in preparation for some lessons I would be teaching the following week. I found myself identifying with poor Antigone as she struggled against the power structures in ancient Greece. Everybody thought they knew what was best for her and kept bossing her around, telling her what to do. I could certainly relate. I finally felt my eyes drooping and was able to close my Kindle and get a few hours of sleep.

It was late afternoon when we arrived in Paris, but with such a short trip we had decided not to stay the night. Rémy rented a car and drove us the 130 kilometers to Rouen and his grandparents' estate, where we would be staying for the next few days.

André, the Giles' majordomo, met us at the door and showed us to our rooms. We showered and unpacked with time to spare before dinner, so I took Jack on a tour of the grounds and gardens. We found a lovely deserted corner and indulged in few moments of the kind of kissing we rarely had time for anymore. It was nice to take a beat and remember that we were newlyweds, after all. On top of the rapidly escalating Seer issues, finishing college, and Jack starting grad school, we had taken on the rearing of a ten year old child. What were we thinking? I sat on my husband's lap, looked into his nearly black eyes, and remembered that I really liked him. He laughed when I told him as much.

"So, what do I need to do to get you to love me? Or should I concentrate on *like like* first?"

I laughed back and leaned in to kiss him on his scruffy jaw. "Oh, I definitely *like like* you. I was going to have Mina slip you a note later. You know, the kind with check-boxes?"

"Well, I'll be sure to check off all the boxes. Who knows? It might help me get lucky later." He retaliated against my kissing, taking over and letting his lips wander over my neck while his hands wreaked havoc under my shirt.

"You might just get lucky right here, mister."

"I like the sound of that," he murmured.

"We do have rooms inside the house, you

know," Rémy said with a chuckle as he rounded the corner into our previously private bower.

I groaned and leaned my head against Jack's chest. "We can't catch a break."

"Get lost, Rémy," Jack growled. "Don't you have a wife of your own? Go kiss her and leave us alone."

"She is napping. I just came to tell you that Geneviève and Arnaud have arrived. But carry on. I'm sure they'll understand," he said and walked away, laughing.

I jumped off Jack's lap and grabbed his hand. "Oh, I can hardly wait for you to meet her! Come on!"

Dinner was a lively affair as we caught up with everything that had been happening in our respective lives over the past few months. Geneviève was almost five months along and starting to show an adorable baby bump.

"We had an ultrasound yesterday," she began, casually cutting into her chicken cutlet.

"And?" Kate asked, setting down her wine glass and leaning forward. "Could they tell what it is?"

"It's…a baby, Grandmére," Geneviève said mischievously.

"Hilarious," Kate said dryly. "You've married quite the comedienne, Arnaud."

"That she is." He laughed and stood up, raising his glass. "I would like to offer a toast to my son. It's a boy." He grinned hugely and accepted good-natured backslapping from Phillipe, Rémy, and even Jack.

I pushed back from the table and rushed to hug

Geneviève, rocking her back and forth. "Oh, I'm so happy for you!" I cried. "All your dreams are coming true, aren't they?"

"Yes, they are. Yours too, no? You have married your Jack and he is every bit as handsome as you described. Maybe you too, will have an exciting addition to your family soon?"

I backed away, my hands in front of me. "Whoa, there, crazy! I'll let you handle the childbearing for now. Give us a few years, okay? I'm only 20. Plus, we are raising Jack's sister, you know."

"I heard. That is so sweet! Okay, I'll give you a couple years before I start nagging about you giving our son a playmate."

Kate had André bring in a bottle of champagne for more toasts and he passed out the flutes—ginger ale for the expectant mother—before joining us in a toast.

Kate waited until after dinner to bring up the true reason for our visit and we spent the next hour or so planning how the newest prophecy 'reveal' would go down the following day. I had wondered about having Phillipe make up a new prophecy for me to say, but Kate already felt bad about the first made up prophecy I'd had earlier in the summer in order to stage the ascension.

"These are my people," she ground out. "I am still responsible for them until the fates or whatever deem it time to reveal the true identity of the new Oracle. I will not have them lied to again."

"What if there is no new Oracle?" I whispered as I stood and looked out the window in the sitting room where I'd once destroyed an heirloom

Meissen vase.

"What?" Phillipe had heard me. "What did you say, Ally?"

I turned and cleared my throat. "What if there is no new Oracle?" I looked around at their blank faces, all except Jack's, whose showed nothing but concern for me. "It's what we're all thinking, isn't it? It may not be me. It may not be anyone. What happens then?"

"I don't know, cherié." Rémy came to stand in front of me and took my hands in his. "You're the only one around here who has, so far, foretold the future." He smirked in the old way that used to annoy me so much. Now it comforted and even amused me.

I managed a small chuckle, which turned into a small sob. "But what about Luc? He'll never stop!"

"Hey." He pulled me into his arms and rubbed my back. "We will stop him. I promise. I have a plan, so trust me, okay?"

"You have a plan? What is it? Tell us."

"Tomorrow. After the big reveal, okay? We'll have plenty of time to talk then."

***

The members of the Conseil gathered mid-morning with plenty of time for the buffet luncheon Kate had planned afterward. She had orchestrated the meeting to include me making a dramatic entrance, standing before them, and reciting the prophecy that she had actually had. I had changed her plans slightly: Jack and I walked in together, holding hands. Oracle or not, the Conseil had better get used to seeing him at my side. I recited the words I had memorized:

Light and dark will battle for preeminence. An ancient evil will return. Darkness shrouds the origins. Blood will be the price.

When I finished, Jack and I took the seats that had been reserved for us and listened while the other Seers in the room discussed possible meanings of this newest, darkest prophecy. I had nothing to add, so I tried to listen, but found my attention wandering. I couldn't get the vision, the conversation with an older Kai, out of my mind. I was nearly frantic with worry over Megan's safety and couldn't find it in myself to care much about prophecies and Oracles.

The endless meeting finally wrapped up and we went in to lunch. I pushed the food around on my plate and gave monosyllabic answers to questions. The others soon gave up and left me alone. I felt Jack's hand squeeze mine and I smiled at him gratefully.

"All right." He stood up and held out his hand to me. "Ally and I are going to our room. We'll see you at dinner."

Sometimes it was nice to have someone take charge.

***

I felt refreshed and slightly calmer after a long

bubble bath and a nap. Jack was amazing, cosseting and spoiling me, even making arrangements for us to have a private dinner in our room. The rest of the Conseil members finally left and we met with Kate, Phillipe, Rémy, and Mina in Kate's private sitting room.

"Okay, what is your plan?" I asked Rémy. "You've kept us waiting long enough."

"Patience, cherié." He stood in front of the rest of us as we were seated on the sofa and easy chairs. "I have given this much thought and I believe it is time to force Luc's hand. We know he is in the United States, most likely in Albuquerque, and most likely watching us."

"What about Kai? What does he have to do with all this? What about my visions? What about Megan?" I choked as I said her name.

"Kai is part of this, I'm sure of it." He ran his hands through his hair in frustration. "But I have no idea why or how. I fear Luc may try to use him if he discovers him, if he discovers that he has any sort of power. This is why I believe we must take action sooner rather than later."

"And you think you know how best to do this?" Phillipe asked.

Rémy nodded. "I propose we draw him out. It's Ally he wants, but she is carefully guarded and rarely alone. What if Mina and I decide to remain in France for a few days longer than Jack and Ally? Maybe a week, as I have many business dealings to attend to. Then Jack will be required to attend one of his army training weekends and Ally will be alone."

"What about Megan?" I asked.

"She will need to remain with her aunt and uncle until this is over. We can't risk her safety."

"I agree. I don't want her anywhere near—"

"No." Jack's voice was low and dangerous.

"Jack, I understand how—" Rémy attempted to placate.

"No." Jack stood and walked across the room to Rémy. "You're talking about using her as bait."

"We will be nearby, all three of us, Jack. She won't really be alone."

"There is no *fucking* way you are going to use my wife as bait for a killer!"

"But she's not *only* your wife, Jack! She is the most powerful Seer in many generations. And she is the Oracle!"

"I don't hear you offering up your own wife as bait!"

"My wife is not the Oracle!"

"You don't know for sure that mine is, either!" He grabbed Rémy by the front of his shirt and shook him. "She's just a girl."

Rémy, to his credit, didn't react; he let Jack shake him until Mina and I intervened. She placed her hands on both men, trying to calm them with her gift.

"Jack, no! Please!" I managed to pry his hands from Rémy's shirt. "It's okay, Jack. This is the best way. Can't you see? We have to keep Megan safe and this is the best way. We need to get this over with so we can move on with our lives. Please, Jack. Just listen."

He took my face in his hands and stared

intensely into my eyes. "I've almost lost you three times, Ally. I can't go through it again. Please don't ask me to do that."

"You're not going to lose me. I swear. And we're not going to lose Megan. This time we will have the upper hand. We will be in control." I could say it, but I wondered if anyone in the room believed it. "Let's just listen to the plan, okay? Please?"

He rested his forehead against mine and squeezed his eyes closed. He nodded and said, "I'll listen. That's all I'm promising."

I led him back to the sofa and held his hand as we listened to Rémy detail his plan. He and Mina would remain in Rouen, purportedly to allow Rémy to attend to some family business. They would attend a society soirée where they would talk *ad nauseam* about their plans for a trip to Marseille as a sort of delayed honeymoon. They would actually return to Albuquerque after the party, using fake passports and flying into Los Angeles and then driving to New Mexico. They would hole up in a house on the block behind ours that he had already rented, in another name, of course. Jack would get a phone call informing him that he was needed to fill in at a special leadership conference because someone had fallen ill. He would leave Friday morning, be seen entering the conference center, and then make his way back to the rented house. Megan would remain with Manny and Trina through the week. Jack would tell them that since he was going out of town, we needed them to keep her for a few days longer.

Jack shook his head as Rémy finished. "No. Not good enough. I need to be in the house with Ally. I can sneak in."

"Luc will know. We can't risk it. It will be difficult enough to get you into the rental house without being seen," Rémy argued.

"Shit! I hate this!" Jack stood again to pace. He shoved his hands through his hair. "Okay, okay. How do we make sure we know what's happening with Ally?"

Rémy just tapped his head. "Mina and I will know. We will be in constant communication."

Jack paced for another minute. "Okay, but I'm going to have Trina and Manny take Megan out of town for the weekend."

"How are you going to convince them to do that?" I asked.

"I don't know!" he roared. "But I'll figure something out! Sorry," he said a beat later.

I crossed to him and put my arms around his waist. "It's going to be okay, Jack. Trust me. I'm psychic." I smiled up at him. "Too soon?"

He laughed mirthlessly and pulled me close. "*Shit*," he muttered again.

Our lovemaking that night was especially intense and perhaps tinged with desperation; afterward we held each other, listening to the silence of the large house echoing around us.

"I need this to be over, Jack."

"I need to know you're going to be safe, querida. I can't agree to this crazy plan of Rémy's if I don't have some assurance of your safety. I want to be there with you, at the house."

The memory of Michael falling into my arms, gunned down by one of Luc's henchmen, flashed through my mind. The thought of Jack being anywhere near me when I finally faced Luc left me cold with terror. I swore to myself that I would meet Luc one final time and I would end this, whatever it took. I realized that Jack didn't know the extent of my powers since I had spent so much time training during the summers when we were apart.

"You know that won't work." I propped myself up on my elbow and stared down at his handsome face. "I can take care of myself, Jack. I'm not afraid of Luc. I'm ready to face him, to deal with this and end it once and for all." I swirled my fingers through the dusting of black hair on his chest.

"Ally—"

"Shh." I leaned forward to kiss him. "I'll show you tomorrow."

"Oh, you'll show me, huh?" He chuckled, sensing my need to put the seriousness behind us for the moment.

"I can be very persuasive, you know." I waggled my eyebrows suggestively.

He laughed, which was maybe not the reaction I was looking for, but it would do. He pulled my face to his, kissed me sweetly, and then rolled me over. "Show me."

Chapter Eleven

"So here I am, against my will and yours too, well I know—no one wants the man who brings bad news."
—*Sophocles, Antigone*

I thought I wouldn't be able to sleep a wink on the flight home, but I closed my eyes soon after takeoff and didn't wake until Jack gently shook me.

"Oh, my God. Did I sleep the whole way?" I asked, yawning. "I'm so sorry, hon."

"Why are you apologizing? I take it as a compliment for keeping you awake last night." He kissed me briefly. "They're bringing breakfast in a minute and you slept through dinner. You need to eat."

I smiled and kissed him back. I appreciated him taking care of me, even though I had taken great pains to assure him that I could take care of myself. Back at the Giles estate, I had taken him into the garden and given a demonstration of the abilities I had worked so hard to refine. I had moved several large boulders around, knocking them together for effect, which caused Rémy to accuse me of being a showoff. Then I had knocked Rémy on his rear end, something I relished doing at any opportunity. Jack was impressed, but still wanted me to carry a gun. I refused, of course. He would have to be satisfied with my crazy psychic abilities and carry the gun himself. Rémy assured him that he and Mina would also be armed.

"Mina has a gun?" I had asked.

"*Mais oui*. She's an excellent shot." He had laughed. "We will take very good care of you, cherié."

I dug into the cheese, baguette, and fruit that the flight attendant placed in front of me, especially relishing the strong, black coffee, and appreciating that Rémy always remembered to order vegetarian meals for me when he made the travel arrangements. Jack slipped his fruit onto my plate and I smiled at him through a mouthful of bread.

We landed in Washington, DC, and had a brief layover before our flight to Albuquerque. By the time we landed, gathered our luggage, and found our car, it was nearly midnight. I breathed a sigh of relief when we finally pulled into our driveway. We headed straight to bed since we both had work and school the next day. Jack had called to check on Megan before we boarded in DC and got the report that she was fine. It had been hard for Jack to hint to Trina that he and I needed some couple time without Megan, but he had done it to keep her safe. We had arranged for Tara and Mat to take her on a road trip to Las Cruces on Saturday morning since

Jack was determined to get her out of town while Luc was likely to act.

I returned home Tuesday evening, after my late class to find Jack sitting at the kitchen table, which was covered with newspaper, cleaning his gun. I set my bag down and hugged him from behind. "Mmmm. You smell good." I kissed his upturned lips. "Cleaning your gun again?"

"Hey, babe. I'm uh, actually cleaning *your* gun."

"My what? I don't have a…oh, Jack," I sighed.

"Please, Ally. I need you to do this."

So, knowing it would make him feel marginally better about Rémy's crazy plan, I sat and learned how to put my new Ruger 9mm together, break it down, and put it together again. And again. It was a small model that fit my hands better than his gun, but it didn't change the fact that I hated guns. It was the only way Jack would agree to wait in the rental house with Rémy and Mina however, so I sucked it up and learned how to use it. After endless rounds of breaking it down and putting it back together, Jack announced that we were going to the indoor shooting range. I swallowed my irritation and played his game. I was a terrible shot; even my normal competitive nature was no match for my lousy skills on the shooting range.

"Hey, I think you hit the target that last time," said Jack as he pressed the button to bring the target back to us. "Yeah, look at that!"

"Where?"

"Right there at the edge. Good job, babe."

I rolled my eyes and demanded food. He laughed good-naturedly and promised that I could choose the restaurant. When I threatened to choose a vegan restaurant, he gulped and said that would be great.

"I'm just kidding. Let's go to that burger joint we tried last week. They do a pretty good quinoa burger."

"Oh, thank God," he said. "I really didn't relish the thought of choking down some of that fake shrimp. That stuff's just vile."

He took me shooting every afternoon that week and I got to where I stopped jerking the gun when I fired and was able to hit the target most of the time. On Thursday evening we stopped by to visit Megan. We missed her terribly and wanted to assure her we would get her back as soon as possible.

"Meg, you know we want you with us, right?" We were ostensibly tucking her in and listening to her read a chapter from her book.

"I know." She nodded. "You and Ally aren't really fighting, are you?"

"No, sweetie. It's Seer stuff. There's just some bad stuff going on right now and we need to know you're safe here with Manny and Trina. It'll be over soon. I promise. Then you can come home where you belong," Jack said as he pulled her comforter around her slim shoulders.

"You guys will be careful, won't you?"

"Of course we will," I said and leaned down to kiss her forehead. "I'll keep your big brother safe, don't worry."

She giggled. "Good. I want to come home soon."

"We want that too, Meg. As soon as possible."

Back downstairs, we patiently listened as Manny and Trina gently lectured us on how difficult the first year of marriage often was and how we needed to be understanding of each other's needs. Trina gave Jack the phone number for a marriage counselor and hinted they would be happy to pay for a few sessions. I knew it cost Jack an immense amount of pride to take the card from his aunt, so I slipped my arm around his waist and hugged him close to my side.

"Thanks, Trina. We'll talk about it, okay? We're doing fine. We just needed a few nights on our own. I am crazy about this guy and wanted him all to myself for a little while. We're thinking that we'll be ready to have Megan back on Sunday night." I hoped I wouldn't have to go back on my words.

We walked out to the SUV silently. Jack started the ignition but didn't slide the gear into drive. "Thanks for that back there, querida. I hate lying to them."

"I know. I am praying this whole thing is over by this weekend. I love you, Jack."

"I know." He gave me a half-smile at our old exchange. "I love you, too."

We were getting ready for bed when I heard from Rémy.

—*We just touched down in Los Angeles and will rent a car and be on the road soon, cherié. How are things there?*

—*Good. Jack bought me a gun and is trying to teach me how to shoot.*

—*God help us all.*

—*Shut up. I'm not that bad.*

"Rémy and Mina are in L.A.," I told Jack. "They'll be on the road soon."

"That still freaks me out a little bit," he said as he crawled under the comforter. "I don't like that he can get inside your head anytime he wants."

"Well, you can get inside much more interesting places than my head," I teased, kissing his neck and working my way down toward his chest.

"You make a good argument." He pulled me on top of him and kissed me deeply. "Ally, it's getting close. I can feel it."

I nodded and stared into his deep brown eyes. "Yeah. It'll be soon. I'm scared, Jack. I want this to be over, but I'm still scared."

"I know, querida. Me too. I have to leave tomorrow and God, I don't want to. You remember to keep the gun with you at all times here at home, right? And make sure you have your phone with you 24/7. Promise me, Ally."

"I promise. I need you to promise me something, okay?"

"Name it."

"Don't talk about it any more tonight. This is our last night together until it's over, hopefully. If we can lure Luc out when I'm alone, then all this can be behind us. Tonight, I need you. Just you. Make love to me, Jack." I leaned forward and kissed him, pleading, promising.

"Of course, babe. Always." He rolled me beneath him and did exactly what I asked.

***

I trudged out to my car Friday after school, exhausted from teaching all day and the stress of this untenable situation. Jack had left early that morning, wearing his fatigues and carrying his duffel bag, and although I knew he was already holed up in the rental house behind ours, I still missed him. Rémy and Mina had arrived a few hours ago and the three of them had set up surveillance on our house, ready to act as soon as Luc showed his face. I really hoped it wouldn't be tonight because I needed to put my feet up and drink a glass of wine before I faced any crazed killers. I wasn't paying attention to my surroundings as I fished my keys from my purse, so I didn't notice the black sedan that was parked next to my SUV.

"Ms. Moran," said a voice from the open passenger window.

I turned toward the black car, dread creeping up my spine and my stomach churning.

"You're going to want to come with me," said the man. He had a heavy French accent, but I had never seen him before.

"Why would I want to do that?" I asked.

Instead of answering, he handed me a cell phone. My hand shook as I raised it to my ear.

"Hello?" I croaked.

"Ally?"

"Megan? Oh my God. Where are you?"

"I don't know." Her voice was so weak. "Kai's dad picked us up after school. He said you told him to. He took us somewhere, I don't know where. He took Kai away. I'm scared, Ally! It's dark here and cold. I'm really sleepy—"

"Ms. Moran." Luc's voice interrupted hers. "I do

hope you'll join us. Your sister-in-law would very much like to see you. Get in the car if you want her to live." The phone clicked off on his end.

The man got out of the front seat, took the phone out of my hand, and opened the back passenger door for me. I looked around the parking lot and noticed a few other teachers walking to their cars, but what help could they give if I screamed? I could get help for myself, but the one truly in danger was Megan. What choice did I have? I trembled as I climbed in the back seat.

"Kai!" I exclaimed when I saw the little boy huddled on the seat next to me.

He turned a tear-streaked face toward me and whispered, "I'm sorry," before turning to the window.

"Hey!" I objected as the man ripped my purse out of my hands and dumped the contents on the seat next to me. I watched as he rooted through makeup, gum wrappers, and tampons to find my cell phone, which he grabbed and shoved into my hands.

"Send a text to the little girl's aunt. Tell her you picked her up from school and are taking her to your home. If you try to send a message to anyone else, the little girl will suffer." I sent the text, although my hands were shaking so hard I had to correct my spelling several times. As soon as I finished, he grabbed my phone, threw it down onto the asphalt of the parking lot, and then stomped it until the screen cracked.

"Bastard!"

The man didn't reply; he simply slammed the car

door in my face and returned to the front seat. As the car accelerated out of the parking lot, I screamed to Rémy in my head.

—*Rémy! Listen, we were wrong! He has Megan! Luc has Megan! He has me too!*

Nothing.

—*Rémy! Can you hear me? Answer me!*

Still nothing. I glanced at the small boy crumpled on the seat next to me and finally understood. It was Kai. When he was around, I couldn't get through to Rémy or Mina. And they couldn't get through to me. Great. Our secret weapon, our one advantage, apparently wasn't so secret after all.

—*Kai. You're doing this, aren't you?* I had no idea if he could hear me or not, but I had to try. *Please, Kai. What is happening? Where is Megan? Is she okay?*

Silence. But I was nearly certain he heard me because his little shoulders tensed.

I gave up for the moment and focused on staring out the window, trying to figure out where we were going. I needed to be able to tell Rémy where to find us as soon as I got the chance. I struggled to keep my tears in as I realized I was completely alone, isolated now, just as I'm sure Luc had planned all along. I was determined not to give him the satisfaction of seeing how upset I was. He had made sure I couldn't tell anyone where I was and had even left my cell phone in the school parking lot so Jack couldn't use the GPS to locate me. Stupid tech-savvy Seers! We drove for several miles, ending downtown behind the rail yards, a hundred year old former Atchison, Topeka, and Santa Fe railway depot. The huge industrial complex was abandoned and in disrepair, but was slated for a major facelift in the near future, part of a downtown urban renewal project.

The man got out of the car and opened my door while the driver opened Kai's. "Let's go," he said and ushered us into the building through a door in a dark alcove in the back of the building.

Inside, the building was dark and cold, the floor littered with broken glass, fast food wrappers, and other unsavory trash. I tripped over a bit of broken brick and fell, scraping my hands and knees, coming within a few millimeters of a discarded hypodermic needle and a used condom. The driver said nothing, just hauled me roughly to my feet and shoved me forward. I sniffed, determined to keep my tears at bay, and followed. We walked for several more minutes, up several flights of stairs, until we emerged on a platform of some sort in the main part of the building with high overhead ceilings and an entire wall of green, brown, and gold stained glass windows, through which the late afternoon sun was struggling to pierce. My heart sank as I recognized the setting of the visions I had been experiencing for months. While it didn't surprise me at all to glimpse the pile of rags up ahead, nevertheless my stomach clenched in dread. Kai cried out and ran to the pile, falling to his knees, his shoulders shaking with his sobs. I was powerless to do anything but creep closer and touch him on one of his heaving shoulders. He turned to me, tears streaming down his face.

"I'm sorry, Ally. I didn't want this. She isn't part of this. I tried to save her, but he made me! I'm so sorry!"

"Kai! What have you done? Is she...?"

"No," he cried as he wiped his eyes. "She's alive. It's you he wants, Ally. He used her to get to you. You have to protect her!"

"I will, Kai. I'll do whatever it takes to keep her safe. I swear it."

"Of course you will. You are extremely predictable, which has made this so much easier." Luc appeared from a side hallway. He was dressed casually, in khaki slacks and a dark red polo shirt, looking more like a Target employee rather than the evil murderer I knew him to be. I really think bad guys should dress like bad guys. He should have been wearing a black suit or something just to make his role in all this very clear. "Ms. Moran, welcome. It seems I finally found the right...motivation, shall we say? I trust I have your undivided attention? My last attempt lacked something, apparently."

"Your last attempt murdered an innocent boy!"

"Simply collateral damage." He shrugged. "You could have prevented his death, if you had only cared enough."

I knew his words were designed to cut deep and they did. They sliced straight into the deep well of guilt I would always carry over Michael's murder. "What do you want?"

"What I've always wanted, Ms. Moran. I want you to work for me, to use your abilities as the Oracle to serve the greater good."

"Whose idea of 'the greater good'? Yours? And

it's Mrs. Ruiz now, actually." I spit the words out through clenched teeth.

"I told you once that your pathetic teenage romance has no place in our world. This supposed marriage of yours is easily put aside. Your place is by my side and far away from this provincial western state. Europe is ours for the taking with your powers and my brilliance. I hope you finally see the immutability of your destiny and the futility of your objections." He gestured to Megan as he spoke.

"Fine. You want me, you got me. Let Megan go. You have to swear she will be okay, that she will be allowed to return to Jack." I choked on these last words, but I was determined to secure her safety. I had no intention of ever going to Europe with crazy, sadistic Luc, but I had to get him to promise Megan would be safe.

"Excellent! That's all I require. It really is very simple. Of course, we will have to dispose of your inconvenient watchdogs first. They have a rather annoying habit of appearing just when they are most unwelcome. Isn't that right, Monsieur Giles?" He turned as he asked his last question, addressing Rémy, who was led into the room and pushed roughly to the ground. The man handed Rémy's gun to Luc, who calmly removed the round in the chamber and pocketed it. He reached behind his back to slide the gun into his waistband. The other man reached down and yanked Rémy to his feet, pressing his gun against his skull.

—Rémy, oh my God! How did you know where I was? How did you find me? Where's Jack?

Nothing. No response. It felt like my thoughts were hitting a brick wall, but I had to try.

As I was attempting vainly to communicate with him, I felt a hard object pressed to the back of my head and heard the hammer of the gun click back. *Crap.* This just kept getting worse. "Really, Luc? Guns? I thought this was my destiny? Why would you need to hold guns on us if I'm destined to do your bidding or whatever?"

"Always so cheeky, Aletheia. We will have to work on your tendency to insolence. I find it extremely fatiguing."

I wanted nothing more than to blast him to smithereens, which I could do, but I couldn't risk it with all the trigger-happy goons holding guns on Rémy and myself.

—Kai. Please, Kai. I know you can hear me. Please help us. Help me help Megan.

He glanced up and met my eyes.

—I knew it! You can hear me. You're blocking Rémy and me, aren't you? Why? What hold does he have over you?

"Ah, I see you have discovered one of my son's many talents," Luc said as he glanced between Kai and me.

His son? Well, I certainly hadn't seen that one coming.

—He is not my father! Kai's voice resonated in my head as he glared at Luc from across the room.

"Kai, you know what I require. Do not disappoint me again, boy." Luc spoke in French, which didn't surprise me. It did surprise me, however, when Kai answered him in kind.

"You promised she would be safe!" His accent was atrocious, but he was definitely fluent, which explained how he had understood when Rémy and I spoke to each other in front of him. My heart sank even further as I realized Luc had always been one step ahead of us. Luc laughed dismissively at the boy's distress.

—*Kai, how did you come to be with him?* Once again, my heart went out to the small boy. *He's horrible! Why do you stay with him?*

—*Do you think I stay from choice? He found me in London, in an orphanage. He brought me here. I have nowhere else to go.*

—*Oh, Kai. I'm sorry. I had no idea.*

—*He only wants you, Ally. If you just go with him he'll leave everyone else alone. Megan will be safe.* He was holding her hand, stroking it as he sent the thoughts at me.

—*Do you really believe that? Do you trust him? I don't. He murdered a friend of mine, Kai. Michael had done nothing. He was simply in Luc's way, so Luc had him killed, right in front of me. Look at him! He has guns aimed at my head and at Rémy's head. He's going to kill him, Kai. He'll most likely kill Megan, too.*

His shoulders drooped. *I know.*

—*Then help me. Stop blocking us. It's the only chance we have.*

—*Okay. But you have to be careful. Luc doesn't know for sure about your abilities, but he suspects. That's why he has been using me.*

—*Can he hear us?*

—*No. But your face doesn't hide your emotions*

well. Your husband is here.

—What? I couldn't turn because of the gun pressed against my skull, but I saw that Kai was staring behind me. I could, however, hear the click of another gun hammer pulled back.

"Drop the gun and move away from my wife *now* or I will blow your fucking head off," Jack growled.

I had never been happier to hear his voice but at the same time wanted him a thousand miles away. I felt the gun removed and breathed a huge sigh of relief. "Jack!" I sobbed and turned to see that he was now holding his gun to the man's head while he kicked the other gun behind him.

"Are you okay?"

"Yeah." I sniffed.

"Go see to Meg. I think she's waking up."

Megan was indeed beginning to stir, so I hurried across the room to her side.

"So, here we all are," Luc began. "We seem to be at something of an impasse. What shall we do? The choice is, of course, yours, Ms. Moran."

I knew he was trying to fluster Jack by using my maiden name, so I sent him an evil look that only made him laugh.

"Ally! You came!" Megan struggled to sit up. "Kai!" She threw her arms around him and hugged him tightly. "Can we go home now? Please?"

"Oh, I'm afraid that is not possible, at least not yet," Luc said. "Ms. Moran has a decision to make first."

—Ally. It was Rémy. The block was gone. *Don't do anything stupid. Get Megan out of here. Jack*

and I can handle Luc. I need you away from here and safe. Mina is waiting outside. Take Megan and go.

—No. He'll kill you. I can't risk it. I looked over at him, where he was being held with a gun pressed against his skull. As I stared, it was as if the rest of the room melted away and all I could see was Rémy. I suddenly knew in the deepest part of my soul that my purpose in life was to protect him in this moment in time. It's what I was born for. I was the Shield, the Protector of Kate's long-ago prophecy. Rémy was the Oracle. The truth of it washed over and through me. *Oh, my God, Rémy! It's you. You are the Oracle.*

His eyes grew large as he realized what I was saying. Then he slammed them shut and hung his head. *How is this possible? How could we have missed this? I feel the truth of it, Ally, but I don't know...*

—I do. My resolve came with the revelation. I absolutely knew what I had to do. *Do exactly what I tell you to, when I tell you to do it.*

"What is your decision, Ms. Moran? I am losing my patience. You either agree to come with me willingly, or your watchdog dies."

"Ally," Jack warned. "Don't even think about it. Just get Meg out of here."

I turned to look at the love of my life, begging him with my eyes to try to understand what I needed to do. *Please, Jack!* I sent the thought at him with every ounce of concentration I could muster, not sure if he would be able to pick up anything. *I have to do this! Please try to understand.*

I turned my thoughts to Kai. *I need your help, Kai. I need you to cause some sort of distraction to draw the attention of the guy holding the gun to Rémy's head, okay?*

—I can do better than that. Tell me when you're ready.

"I can see you have decided to be stubborn about this," Luc said. "Apparently the lives of your friends are meaningless to you. Perhaps the loss of another will help you decide."

"That would be a grave mistake, Luc," I said.

"Oh really? I don't think so," he replied, turning to the man holding the gun on Rémy.

"Wait! Do you really want to shoot the Oracle?"

"What are you talking about?" Luc asked, scoffing.

"The ascension was fake, Luc." I stood slowly. "I'm not the Oracle. Rémy is."

He laughed. "That is ridiculous! You should choose better lies."

"I'm not lying."

"The Oracle cannot be a man. That is impossible!" But I thought I detected a hint of uncertainty in his eyes.

"Oh, yeah? What, is it against the Oracle handbook? Wait—there is no handbook, is there? There really are no rules to this whole Seer business. Who's to say a man can't be the Oracle? Everything's changing, Luc. You can't be sure, can you?"

He was wavering, looking between Rémy and me. I took advantage of Luc's momentary confusion to call out to Kai in my mind. *Ready!*

Kai held his hand toward the man holding the gun to Rémy's head and the gun was suddenly in Kai's hand. He turned to me. *Now!*

Luc started to reach for the gun he had slid into his waistband.

—*Rémy! Duck!* To his great credit, he hit the floor without stopping to ask any stupid questions. I sent a huge blast of energy straight at Luc and the gunman. The gunman flew back off the platform to the brick floor at least twenty feet below. The sound of his head hitting the bricks is something that would haunt me for a long time.

Luc hadn't fallen, but had been knocked against a wall. As he started to regain his feet, he again reached for the gun he had put in his waistband. Rémy tackled him before he could fire and knocked it out of his hands. They began hand-to-hand combat, punching whatever they could reach. Luc was a fierce and dirty fighter, but Rémy was younger. Still, I feared Luc would get to the gun before Rémy had the chance to finish him off.

I turned to see Jack and the man who had held a gun on me fighting, as well. Jack was completely capable and clearly had the upper hand, so I simply ran to retrieve the gun the man had dropped earlier and turned back to help Rémy. The gun was behind them, on the edge of the platform, so I aimed a blast of energy that sent it sailing off the edge and well out reach of Luc.

I searched wildly for Kai and Megan, terrified they would be caught in the middle of one of the fights. I finally spied them in a far corner, Kai huddled over Megan, protecting her. God, I loved that kid in that moment.

Rémy and Luc were still throwing punches, but Luc got in a lucky blow that seemed to daze Rémy. He fell to the ground; Luc took the advantage and kicked him viciously in the ribs, pushing him near the edge of the platform. Rémy screamed in pain. My vision hazed red as Luc drew his foot back yet again, preparing to kick Rémy in the face. I raised my hand and sent another blast of energy that hit Luc square in the back and sent him flying over Rémy to the bricks below.

I thought I heard a cry of some sort from behind me, but I was too busy rushing across the room to Rémy. "Are you okay?" I pulled him up from the floor and threw my arms around him. He squeezed me briefly, clutching his ribs in pain, then set me aside and went to look over the edge of the platform. He turned back to me and shook his head. I pushed the buzzing that was trying to creep in my brain away. I had too much to deal with at the moment.

"Jack?" Megan pushed herself off the floor. "Jack!" She ran across to where he was lying on the ground.

I cried out in horror as I realized he wasn't moving. My legs were rubber as I ran/crawled to where my husband lay crumpled on the floor. "No, no," I whispered in terror as I saw the pool of blood spreading beneath him. So much blood. He was unconscious, his dark face more pale than I ever thought possible. "Oh, God! Please, Jack, please don't do this! Wake up!"

Megan was huddled on the other side of Jack,

crying hysterically. "Kai! Please, Kai! Help him!"

I was unceremoniously shoved out of the way as Kai moved to Jack's side, ripping his shirt up to reveal a gaping wound in his stomach. It looked like he'd been stabbed. Kai placed his hand directly over the hole, closed his eyes, and bowed his head forward, nearly resting it on Jack's chest.

"What in the hell?" Rémy rushed forward.

"No!" Megan screamed and threw herself at him, holding him back by virtue of grabbing ineffectually at his shirt.

"Rémy, let him be!" Mina appeared, blood streaming down her face. Rémy forgot Jack and rushed to her side in time to catch her as she fainted.

I turned back to Jack just as Kai shuddered and sat back. He dropped his bloody hands away from Jack's body and drooped in defeat. *No. Oh, God, no.* I took Kai's place, bending over Jack's too-still form. I took his limp hand in mine and kissed the back of it, the sobs building in my chest, bursting out in a harsh explosion. *Not Jack! Please, not Jack!* How would I live without him? Endless moments passed; the only sound in the entire building was the echoing of the sobs from Megan and me. Then, I felt it: the smallest flutter of movement from the cold hand I held in mine. "Jack?"

He gave a gasp, sucking in air as he struggled to sit up. "Ow!" He grasped his stomach. "What the hell happened?"

"Jack! Oh, my God!" I threw my arms around his neck and sobbed even harder as his arms came around me.

Chapter Twelve

"Love resistless in fight, all yield at a glance of thine eye, Love who pillowed all night on a maiden's cheek dost lie, Over the upland holds. Shall mortals not yield to thee?"
—Sophocles, Antigone

I covered his face with kisses, stopping only when he grabbed my head in his hands.

"I'm okay, babe. I'm okay. My stomach hurts like hell, but I'm okay. What happened?"

"You were stabbed, I think." I tried to speak but was still crying. "Kai. Kai saved you."

As I said his name, the boy sat up and looked to where Rémy was holding an unconscious Mina in his arms. He crawled over to them, wiped Jack's blood on his t-shirt, and placed his hand on Mina's head. He closed his eyes and concentrated for a moment. When her eyelids fluttered, he removed his hand and slumped backward.

"She'll be fine," he murmured. "So will the baby." Then he passed out.

No one said a word; we all simply stared at each other with blank, stupid looks on our faces. Megan ran to her friend while I met Mina's eyes. We slowly smiled in understanding.

"You're...pregnant?" Rémy whispered. He spoke in French and I was certain he didn't realize it. Mina nodded happily. Rémy turned decidedly pale with a tinge of green and Mina wisely pushed his head down between his knees and murmured to him softly.

I helped Jack to his feet as he clutched his stomach. "I'm fine," he groaned. "Call Brian while I get the little guy."

"I have to get my gun," Rémy said as he pushed to his feet, groaning and clutching his side. "They could trace it to me." He disappeared down the stairs to retrieve the gun Luc had taken from him.

An hour later, we were seated in our living room. Kai reclined on the sofa, wearing one of Jack's t-shirts and sipping orange juice, while Rémy sipped a whiskey, both of them slowly regaining their color. I heard the shower shut off and took a glass of whiskey back to the bedroom for Jack. He was wearing a pair of boxers and was sitting on the closed toilet seat, examining the black t-shirt he had been wearing, his finger poking through the knife hole.

"Here." I handed him the drink. "You probably need this."

He looked up at me, took the glass from my hand, and belted it back. "I got stabbed. I should probably be dead."

"I kind of think you were for a minute." I lifted

my trembling hand to my mouth, trying to keep in a sob. I failed. Jack set aside his glass and pulled me to sit on his lap. "I almost lost you tonight," I whispered against his chest.

"But you didn't. I'm still here. I don't know how or why, but I'm still here." He held me as I cried for a few minutes. When I quieted, he stood and moved to the bedroom to get dressed. I sat on the bed, watching him pull on a pair of jeans. As he straightened, I reached out to touch the smooth, unmarred skin of his stomach.

"I owe Kai everything," I whispered. I stood on tip-toe and pulled his beloved face down to mine and kissed him fiercely. "I'm so sorry, Jack. Now I know how you felt when I came close to dying. When I saw you lying there, *lifeless"*—I choked on the last word—"I wanted to die too."

He pulled me close and kissed me just as fiercely. "I know, babe. I know." He held me for a moment. "Is everyone still out in the living room?"

I nodded. "Yeah. Brian will be here soon." I had called him as Jack and Rémy scoured the room at the rail yards, making sure there was nothing that could possibly lead back to any of us.

Kai was looking better, sitting up next to Megan, who hadn't left his side since we got home. I walked over to him, sat beside him, and pulled him into my arms. He seemed shocked and might have resisted had I given him any sort of chance. The power that surged through him, even in his current state of exhaustion, was immense and unlike anything I had ever encountered. This would bear greater examination at a later date, but for now I owed this boy every bit of gratitude I could muster for saving Jack's life.

"Thank you, Kai. Thank you for saving him." He froze for a few seconds then hugged me back tightly. My heart melted as I met Jack's eyes over Kai's head.

Jack knelt in front of him and joined the hug. "Kai. I don't even know how to thank you. I can't even express what I'm feeling right now." His eyes were wet as he closed them, his head resting on top of Kai's. He pulled himself together and stood to shake Rémy's hand. "So, congratulations, Dad. Oh, and on the whole Oracle thing too." I had caught Jack up on what he had missed while he was unconscious during the drive home.

Rémy smiled weakly and then laughed. "I'm going to be a father. Finding out about the Oracle is nothing compared to that."

"That is a very sweet thing to say, love," Mina said as she plopped on his lap. I noticed he grabbed his ribs and winced, trying to hide it from Mina. "That has earned you a kiss, at the very least."

"So, Rémy is the Oracle," Jack began. "And Ally is the Shield. I guess that makes sense, and Mina is definitely the Heart of the Oracle. All this time." He shook his head. "Hey, you okay?" He had turned back to me, knowing me well enough to realize I would be upset that my actions as the Shield had ended the lives of two men tonight.

I nodded as I winced. "I will be. I didn't mean to hurt anyone, but it was a choice between Rémy and them. I had to protect him. I had to. I would do it again if I had to."

"Luc's dead, isn't he?" Kai asked quietly.

I moved back to sit by him, taking his hand. "He is. I'm sorry, Kai."

"I'm not," he said flatly. "I hated him." Then he melted against me, sobbing violently.

"Hey, hey," I soothed, smoothing his blond curls out of his face. "It's okay. It'll be okay." I let him cry it out, which he seemed to need. Jack pushed a tissue in his hand as he began to calm somewhat.

"What's going to happen to me?" he asked as he mopped his face. "I hated him but he was all I had."

"You'll stay with us," Jack stated firmly. "At least until we can figure out what to do. Is that okay?"

Kai nodded. "Yes, sir. Thanks."

Megan stood and hugged her brother. "Thank you, Jack. I love you."

"I love you too, Meg."

Mina had the presence of mind to put together some sandwiches, which Kai and I devoured. Our expenditures of psychic energy earlier had drained both of us. Rémy tried to refuse, opting instead for another whiskey, but Mina firmly took the glass out of his hand and replaced it with a sandwich. He was in too much pain to eat, however, and I offered to get him some aspirin.

Kai threw off the blanket and moved to Rémy's side. "Let me help." He held out his hand toward Rémy's ribs.

"Kai, honey, you need to rest," I objected.

"I'm fine. Please," he insisted.

Rémy reluctantly lifted his shirt and hissed as Kai placed his hand over the red, bruised area. It seemed to cause both of them pain, judging by the grimaces on their faces. It took longer than Jack or Mina's healings and I worried that Kai wasn't up to it. He finally gave a shudder and pulled his hand away.

Rémy caught him before he fell and carried him back to the sofa. "Ally, bring him some more juice, please."

I brought the juice and sat beside the little boy as he drank. "Kai, you need to rest. No more healing tonight, okay?"

"I'll be fine. Bones are harder to heal."

"No kidding," said Rémy. "Be glad you were unconscious, Jack." He rested his hand on Kai's head. "Thank you, little one. You saved me many weeks of pain. But you feel the pain, don't you? You take it into yourself somehow."

Kai nodded and I pulled him into my arms again. Where did this latent maternal instinct come from?

Brian came in a few minutes later and told us that the police were treating the scene as some sort of possible gang violence. Neither Luc nor the other man who had fallen had any sort of identification on them and all of the others had disappeared. He said there didn't appear to be any sign of our presence specifically, just a general appearance of some sort of activity. He would do his best to make sure the case didn't get a lot of time or attention. "Now, I need you all to tell me what the hell really happened tonight."

I began the story, relating how the black sedan had been waiting for me after school and how I had listened to Megan on the phone. "How did you know where to find me?" I asked Jack and Rémy. "They smashed my phone so I know you weren't able to track the GPS. We thought he would try to grab me here at the house."

"I had one of my friends watching you every second I couldn't," Jack said. "There's no way I was going to trust your safety to Rémy's lame-ass plan. He called me the second you got in that car and followed you to the rail yards. We got there just a few minutes after you."

"We decided I would go in first." Rémy took over the story. "They were waiting for me, just inside the door. God, I was wrong about everything." He dropped his head into his hands.

"I followed at a distance and Mina waited outside," Jack explained.

"What happened to you?" I asked Mina. "You were bleeding."

"I was waiting outside, like Rémy ordered. I wasn't happy about it and had just decided to find everyone when the door flew open, right into my head. It knocked me down and I nearly passed out for a minute. I saw a guy running away, but I was too dazed to do anything about it."

"That must have been the one who stabbed you," Rémy said to Jack.

"Yeah, I remember that part. When Ally blasted Luc, I lost my focus for a second. The guy I was fighting pulled a knife and nearly gutted me. That's the last thing I remember."

"You were stabbed?" Brian nearly yelled. "Where? Why aren't—"

"Brian," I interrupted. "You should probably sit

down for this next part. You aren't going to like it."
He sat as I told him, as gently as possible, about
how Kai had healed Jack, then Mina, and finally
Rémy a few minutes ago. He paled noticeably as he
glanced over at the little boy sitting on the couch
next to Megan.

"Oh, my God," he mumbled.

I was about to answer, to try to offer some sort of
comfort, when the air in the room began to crackle
with energy. I looked around, startled, and saw
Rémy rise to his feet, his eyes glazed over, and a
visible aura of energy surrounding his body.

*"This is the first prophecy of the new age. The
power of the three is now complete. The Oracle is
now ascended. The former age will fade away. The
Light has overcome, but the Darkness is not
defeated. The child is the key."*

No one said a word; we just stared at Rémy. The
glow faded and his eyes returned to normal. Mina
finally launched herself into his arms and they held
each other tightly. "You *are* the Oracle," she
whispered.

"I am," he whispered back.

"I need to write it down," I murmured. "I hope I
remember what he said." I got up to find a pen and
pencil.

"Don't worry, cherié," Rémy said. "I heard it. I
remember what I said."

"Well, that's different. Kate never knows what
she says," I mused. "You heard what you said and
you remember?"

He nodded. "I have a feeling everything will be different this time." His phone rang as he spoke. "That's Grandmére," he said without looking. "She knows."

While he talked to his grandmother, I poured a couple fingers of whiskey for my poor stepfather, who was valiantly trying to deal with the events of the evening. He drank a sip or two but then set it aside, saying he needed to drive home.

"I'm going to go home and try to forget all this," he said as he gestured around the room. "For God's sake. I have no idea what I'm going to do about my report." He hugged me and kissed my forehead. "Are you going to be okay, Ally? This is all just crazy."

"Yeah, I'll be fine. I'm used to crazy. Go home, Brian. Mom and Eli need you."

Later that night, after Brian had returned home to my mother and my brother, after Rémy and Mina had gone back across the street to their home to revel in the news of their impending parenthood and try to digest the fact that Rémy was the Oracle, after Megan was tucked in her bed and Kai was settled in the guest room, Jack and I held each other in the dark as we lay in bed.

"Is it really over, Jack?"

I felt him nod. "Please, God. Ally, how do you feel about not being the Oracle? Are you okay with it?"

I pulled away, leaning on my elbow and looking deeply into his beautiful eyes. "I can't even begin to express how relieved I am. Rémy will be a much better Oracle than I ever would have been. Jack, we can have a normal life." I kissed him. "Well, at least a semi-normal life. I'm still psychic."

He laughed and pulled me to lie on top of him. "I'm okay with that, crazy psychic girl." He kissed me, brushing my hair behind my ears. "And there is the whole issue of acquiring another kid tonight. Rémy and Mina are going to have a baby, but we've suddenly got two kids. I have a feeling he's going to be with us permanently."

"Look who's psychic now. I couldn't possibly be any more in love with you than I am at this moment," I whispered against his lips. "I think Kai needs us."

"Yeah, probably. He and Megan sure have some kind of connection, huh?"

"Yeah, they sure do. I'm not sure how I feel about it."

"Me neither. It kind of gives me the creeps, to tell you the truth," he said.

"Yet you opened our home to him anyway. That's why I love you." I kissed him, running my hands across the smooth skin of his stomach where, a few hours ago, a knife wound had nearly taken his life. I curled against him and we both fell asleep.

***

I woke up early Saturday morning and checked on the kids on my way to the kitchen. I had a moment of panic when I found Megan's bed empty, but managed to keep my cool while I checked on Kai. He was still sound asleep, as were Megan and Sodapop, who were curled up at the end of his bed, the dog snoring loudly. I rolled my eyes and let them sleep. I would need to have a talk with Meg about it at some point in the near future, but for now I left them alone.

Rémy let himself in the back door as I was making coffee. He walked straight to me and pulled me into his arms, hugging me tightly. "Oh, my God, Ally. It's over. Finally."

I hugged him back, knowing how difficult this last year had been for him as he worked vainly to find out where Luc was while worrying about trying to keep Mina and me safe. "It is, but I have a feeling there is a bunch of new stuff on the horizon. Your prophecy certainly seemed to intimate as much."

"Damn prophecy," he groused. "They're never much good, are they? Just vague, threatening crap."

I laughed. "You sound like me. Hey, I haven't had a chance to congratulate you yet, Papa. How is the little mama doing?"

He sighed in a delirious sort of way. "Ah, she is perfect. She's not feeling terribly well this morning, though. I was actually hoping you might have some crackers I could take to her."

Jack appeared at that moment, shirtless and hair mussed. "Should I be worried?" he asked, not sounding the least bit upset as he reached around us for the coffee pot.

"Not in the slightest," Rémy chuckled as he hugged me again and then let me go. "I just came over to borrow crackers for my pregnant wife. Oh, God, my wife is pregnant." He reached blindly for a chair, noticeably pale. "How did this happen?"

I met Jack's amused gaze as I helped Rémy sit in

a chair before he passed out. "The usual way, I'm pretty sure. Here, drink this." I set the cup of coffee that Jack handed me in front of Rémy. "You're going to be a great dad. Congratulations." I kissed the top of his head and then ruffled his hair.

I managed to get him to drink half a cup before he took the crackers and rushed back to Mina, promising to return later to help us figure out what our next steps were in regard to Kai. In spite of the craziness of the day before, or maybe because of it, I was determined to make this as normal a morning as possible. I fixed pancakes while Jack fried bacon, the smell of which drew the two children to the kitchen. Kai was quiet during breakfast, but easier around us than he had ever been. I had many questions for him, but decided they could wait as we enjoyed our first breakfast together as a family.

We left Megan with Mina later that morning while Jack, Rémy, and I drove Kai to the house he had lived in with Luc and the nanny. The two men left us in the car while they approached the house cautiously, unsure of what or whom they would find. Jack appeared at the car a few minutes later.

"It's empty. Looks like someone left in a hurry. Bring Kai."

We followed the boy into what had been his bedroom. It and the entire house looked like it had been hastily furnished by a service of some sort; there were absolutely no personal touches anywhere. Kai said nothing as he emptied the drawers and closet of the pitifully few clothing items provided for him. It nearly broke my heart to see the only personal decorative items in the entire house sitting on his dresser—the ceramic cat and the saltshaker shaped like a fox missing from my kitchen.

"I stole those. I'm sorry," he whispered. "I just wanted—" He broke off and shrugged. He held his hand out toward them and the cat flew across the room and into his palm. He held the other hand out and pulled the saltshaker across the room, as well. I had seen this power of his the night before when he took the gun away from Rémy's captor, but it still amazed me. What in the world *was* Kai? What else could he do? But these questions would need to wait; right now we had a lonely, scared little boy on our hands.

I crossed the room and crouched in front of him. He placed the two items in my hands. I bit my lip and looked at Jack, who also shrugged. "Here." I handed him the cat figurine. "How about a compromise? You keep the cat, but we really need our salt shaker back." I smiled as I said it.

He looked at me with his brilliant green eyes brimming over. He carefully took the cat out of my hand and then threw his arms around me.

***

"Do you have any idea whether or not you have a birth certificate?" Rémy asked. We were seated around our kitchen table, trying to figure out the legalities—or ways around them—of having Kai live with us.

Kai shook his head. "I don't know. I don't think so. I hadn't been at the orphanage long before Luc showed up."

"How did you get to the orphanage? What happened to your parents, sweetie?" I asked, reaching out to place my hand over his. I was glad that he seemed not to mind being touched now that we all knew about his powers.

He shrugged. "I don't know. I don't remember them, except for some vague memories. My mother was beautiful. I think she's dead," he whispered. "I lived with some people but they were pretty mean to me, so I ran away and lived in an alley, in a cardboard box for a while." He stopped at my gasp, but shrugged off the horrors of his childhood in his usual stoic manner. "Anyway, I was picked up by the police for stealing food and ended up at the orphanage. I had a bunch of foster parents, but they never lasted long. Stone isn't my real last name. It's just the name of the last family I lived with. I don't remember my real last name." He reached into his shirt and pulled out a ring of some sort hanging from a long chain. "This is the only thing I have left from my parents." He handed it to me.

I examined the heavy gold ring. It appeared to be a man's ring with a dark red stone in the middle and some sort of markings on the band. I handed it to Rémy. "Well, you're with us now. Are you okay with that?" I asked.

He nodded. "I want to be with Megan. I'll try not to be too much trouble. I promise I won't steal any more."

And my heart melted the rest of the way. I pulled the little boy onto my lap and hugged him. After a moment he relaxed in my arms. "Hey, for whatever reason, you're part of our family now. We may not be the best parents in the world, but we'd like to be yours."

"I'd get to live here from now on? And Megan would be my sister?"

"Technically, since she's my sister," Jack said as he handed Kai's ring back to him, "She would be your aunt."

Both Megan and Kai found this hilarious. We sent them off to play while we hashed out the details with Rémy. They were still laughing and Kai was calling her 'Auntie Meg.' I didn't care why; I was thrilled to hear the too-serious little boy laughing.

"Is there any way to make this happen?" Jack asked. "The kid doesn't even have a birth certificate."

"Of course it's possible," Rémy said. "The first hurdle will be the birth certificate. Then we will acquire adoption papers. It should be done within a month or two at the most."

"I don't suppose there's any normal, legal way to do it?" I asked.

"It will be perfectly legal, but normal would be extremely problematic." Rémy shook his head. "You and Jack are not nearly old enough to legally adopt anyone, much less a ten year old child, if that's even his real age. For that and many other reasons, I think it will be much better to do it quietly. Once I have the papers, I will have an attorney deliver copies to the school."

"How much will this cost us?" Jack asked, a worried look on his face.

Rémy brushed his question away while he packed away the notes he had been taking. "It will be taken care of. He is a Seer and part of our world."

"But what else is he?" I asked. "He's so much more than a Seer."

"That I don't know, cherié. Time will tell, I suppose. For now, a lonely little boy has a good home."

So Kai settled into life with the Ruizes. It was a surprisingly smooth transition, probably because he was ridiculously eager to please us. He never complained about doing homework or chores, often completing Megan's chores as well as his own. I tried to talk to him about this, but he continued to try and make her life as easy as possible, even though she swore she never asked him to. In return, I noticed she made him frequent treats, maybe trying to fatten him up a bit. He finally started to fill out slightly, the result of three good meals a day and a lot less stress in his life. He was still an extremely quiet child, however, seeming to need more time alone than most kids his age. He enjoyed reading and devoured nearly all the books on Megan's shelves, with the exception of the ones he labeled as 'too girly.' He loved our weekly trips to the public library. He also loved Sodapop, spending hours throwing sticks for him in the backyard and taking him for long, daily rambles. I worried about him, wondering if we should get him into counseling, but Grams and Jack advised simply giving him some time to acclimate to living with a normal—if we could be considered anything near normal—family for a while. My side of our extended family, as well as Mat and Tara, helped us with the story we created for Jack's side of the family: Kai was the son of a distant cousin of Grams' from England whose parents had been killed in a car accident. He and Megan had immediately bonded, and Jack and I decided it would be better for him to live with us.

"Well, I'm not sure that's a good idea," Trina worried when she first found out. "You and Ally are so young and just starting married life. You've already taken on a huge responsibility with Megan. Can't he live with Ally's mother?"

Jack assured her we wanted him with us. We tried to convince Kai himself of the same thing.

We finally got a chance to sit him down and ask about his powers. We had wanted to make sure he felt comfortable before we grilled him, so it was several weeks into our new family arrangement.

"So, how long have you known about your abilities?" I asked. "Did they come gradually?"

He shrugged in his quiet way. "I've always had them, I guess. I can't remember not having them."

"What about the healing? How did you know about that?" I continued to prod.

"I figured it out when I was about five. Any time I hurt myself, like a scrape or a cut, it healed really fast. I didn't know I could do it to other people until Megan. I'd never tried before." I remembered how fast his black eye had healed after the fight at school.

"But it exhausts you, doesn't it?" I rubbed the back of his hand, still amazed by the amount of power I could detect flowing through him.

He nodded.

"Tell me about the dreams, Kai."

"I don't know. I just think about a person while they're sleeping and I'm in their dreams. Luc made me go into Megan's dreams and become friends with her to spy on you. But she was nice to me. I didn't want to spy on you. I'm so sorry, Ally."

"Oh, Kai. I know. Please don't worry about that anymore. Do you have any idea why you were older when you invaded my dreams and that time in the vision?"

He shook his head. He looked miserable and I wished we could bring this conversation to a halt, but I didn't want to revisit it any time soon, so I plowed forward.

"Is there anything else you can do? Anything we don't know about?" I asked gently.

He sighed and reached his hand out toward the hallway. Within seconds, one of his notebooks appeared. He tore a piece of paper out and handed it to me. I stared at it blankly, wondering what he was trying to show me. Then words started to appear on the paper. They were in his childish handwriting:

I guess you could consider this as another power. Kind of useless, huh?

"Oh, my God, Kai!" I exclaimed.

"Holy shit!" muttered Jack.

"I think it's cool!" Megan staunchly defended him.

"Of course it's cool," I said as I gave Jack a dirty look. "It just surprised us, that's all. I'm sure there's a purpose for it. Grams always says power is given to help others. But you are not to use it to help Megan on a test, is that clear?"

The children exchanged guilty glances, so I assumed I had guessed correctly. As they left the room together I could hear Megan muttering to him. "You had to show her, didn't you? You could have kept that last one a secret." Kai smiled and shook his head.

Rémy was as good as his word and in just over a month, right before the Christmas holidays, we had paperwork—which he assured us would hold up to the closest scrutiny—declaring Kai to be our son. We kept it secret until that evening. I helped Jack prepare Kai's favorite meal so far, spaghetti with meatballs, and his favorite dessert, chocolate ice cream with colorful sprinkles.

"Oh, boy! Spaghetti and meatballs! My favorite! Thanks! What's this?" He gestured to the beautifully wrapped gift next to his plate.

"Open it," I said, barely able to contain my own excitement.

He reached for the gift hesitantly. I realized he probably hadn't opened very many gifts in his life. He carefully slit the tape on one end and began unfolding the paper.

"Just rip it!" Megan exclaimed, bouncing in her seat. She was in on the surprise, but had sworn to keep the secret.

"Let him be, brat. He can open his presents any way he wants," Jack said, laughing.

Kai finally finished unwrapping, opened the box, and folded back the tissue paper. He picked up the small silver key chain with our house key and examined it. "Kai Stone-Ruiz," he read on the engraved surface. Although he had said Stone was not his real last name, we felt it was important to keep some part of his past intact. He clutched it as he pulled the orange and blue jersey out of the box. It had Stone-Ruiz across the back shoulders. Kai loved American football, and much to Jack's dismay, was a huge Broncos fan. Jack hated the Broncos. He looked up at us, concern written across his features. "The papers came?"

"The papers came," Jack agreed. "You're officially part of this family. As officially as we can make it, anyway. But Kai, it's real to us. You need to know that."

"Wow," Kai whispered. "You're my parents now."

"Yeah, we are," Jack said. "And you're our son."

Kai carefully set the keychain and jersey down and walked around to Jack's chair. "Can I call you Dad?" he asked, whispering.

Jack met my eyes, his own suddenly wet. "I'd sure like that." He pulled our son into his arms.

I, of course, started bawling.

"I think your mom could use a hug," Jack said.

Few things in my life had ever been as sweet as holding my new son in my arms. "I love you, Kai. I'm so glad you're my son," I whispered against his hair.

"I love you too, Mum. I don't think I've ever said that before," he admitted. "Either part: the love or the Mum."

I laughed and held him tighter. "Well, I hope you

say it a lot."

Later that night, Jack and I stood in the doorway of our son's bedroom and watched him sleep. Megan was, of course, curled up at the foot of the bed. I had spoken to her, but she still couldn't bear to let him out of her sight for an entire night, so we let it go for now.

"Our kids are beautiful, Jack," I said, curling my hand into his.

"Yeah," he said. "I never thought I'd have two kids by the time I was 22."

"At least we don't have to change their diapers."

"That would be awkward." He laughed softly.

"Jack," I drew him across the hall to our own bedroom and shut the door. "Four years ago, you pulled me out of my seat in our English class and dragged me to the girl's bathroom." I pulled his face down and kissed him. "I walked out of that bathroom and saw you leaning against the wall, looking so handsome and sexy I could have died. I never dreamed I would be with you, like this, in our bedroom with our two kids across the hall. I'm so incredibly happy. I love you so much."

"Ally," he sighed against my lips. "You are my life, querida. I thank God every day that I had the good sense to drag you to that bathroom. I fell in love with you when you walked into physics class the first day of our junior year. Don't laugh! It's true. I knew you were the one for me, but I was never going to talk to you."

"That would have been a damn shame," I said as I unbuttoned his shirt. I pushed the shirt off his shoulders and leaned in to kiss his chest. "What changed your mind?" At his confused look, I continued. "Why did you decide to talk to me, after all those months of sitting behind me, giving me the silent treatment?" We both laughed and I kissed him again.

"You want to know why?" He scooped me up in his arms as I nodded. "Because you needed me. I never would have talked to you if you hadn't needed me."

"Oh, Jack. I did need you. I still do. I always will. Especially right now." We both laughed softly. "But more than that, I want you, every day, in my life. I love you, Jack Ruiz."

"And I love you, Ally Moran-Ruiz." He kissed me as he set me down on the bed.

Epilogue

"Leave me to my own absurdity."
—*Sophocles, Antigone*

5 Years Later

"Come on, Ally! Push! You can do it, babe!"

"Jackson Ruiz, if you tell me to push one more time, I'm going to make you wish—"

"Okay, sorry! I'm teasing. Come over here and hold the baby. I'll be happy to take over! You're the one who insisted on mowing the lawn all by yourself."

"Ugh!" I screamed and gave up on the cantankerous lawnmower, which had died as I tried to push it through a patch of especially long grass. "Tell me again why we can't get an electric lawnmower?"

"Because I don't want to make it too easy for you to mow the lawn, querida. Kai and I can handle this one. You have enough to do without yard work."

"Okay, fine, but I just wanted to prove that I'm more than the Jersey cow I sometimes feel like." I stalked across the lawn to take our three-month old daughter out of Jack's arms. "Come here, angel." I kissed her sweet-smelling head as she nuzzled close, smelling my milk.

"You don't begin to resemble a Jersey cow," Jack said as he kissed the top of my head and then the baby's. "But I love how big your—"

"Jack!" I threatened.

"Sorry," he said, laughing and not sounding sorry at all. "Ah, saved by the bell." Kai and Megan arrived home from school just then. "Kai, your mom was trying to mow the lawn. I told her to wait until you got home, but she just wouldn't listen."

"Oh, and what's wrong with you?" Megan laughed and jumped on Jack's back. "Did you break your arm?"

"Oof!" he groaned. "No. Your niece is keeping me up most of the night. I thought I'd take a nice little nap while Kai mows the lawn."

"I got it, Dad," said Kai as he started the mower on the first try, damn him.

"Kai! I'm kidding! I just wanted to see how far your mom would take it. I'll mow the lawn." Jack detached Megan from his back and walked across the lawn. I could see my husband and son arguing good-naturedly over who would finish the chore.

"Come inside, Ally," Megan said. "Olivia needs her afternoon snack. I'll get you some juice. Then I may take a nap, because that baby is keeping all of us awake. I saw Mina on the way over. She said you invited them to dinner and she said she's bringing dessert. It'll be nice to spend some time with the twins and Océane." Rémy and Mina had augmented their family with twin sons almost a year ago. Their adorable daughter was nearly four years old and Megan loved her. Rémy had taken his place as the new Oracle, but was determined to do things his own way. He had declared that it was far past time for the two Seer groups to reunite and begin working together, making sure nothing like Luc and *Les Dépaysés* ever had the chance to gain power again. He had also decided that the new Oracle should live in America and was working to create an American Seer Council, headed by none other than Cassie, my former mentor. I hadn't seen much of her since I graduated from high school and looked forward to spending time with her on council issues. He and Mina still lived across the street from us, although I knew they could well afford a much nicer house. Somehow the three of us—Rémy, Mina, and I—felt more comfortable living in close proximity. He and Mina traveled frequently to France and Ireland, or at least they had until the twins were born. Kate continued to thrive, although she was starting to slow down some, but her prophecies had ground to a halt within a year of Rémy's ascension. She assured us she was happy with this development and it was really like being retired.

"Mat and Tara are coming too. They're bringing a salad. I'm making pasta. I'll get it started as soon as I finish feeding Olivia." Tara was expecting their first child in less than a month. They'd had a heartbreaking miscarriage a year and a half earlier and were nervous and excited for this baby. Tara was planning to take a leave of absence from her job at the Albuquerque Police Department crime lab for at least six months as soon as the baby arrived. I had taken a year off from teaching in order to be with our daughter full-time and loved it, although I missed my classroom. Jack had finished his stint with the army and was working for Sandia National Laboratories as a mechanical engineer, a job he loved and which afforded us a very comfortable lifestyle. We had lived in Germany for a year during his time on active duty and then he had done a nine-month tour of duty in Afghanistan while the kids and I returned home. Kai and Megan had been the only thing that kept me sane during that awful time. We had conceived Olivia soon after he returned home, possibly that very night.

I settled into the rocking chair that Jack had bought when we found out I was pregnant and settled my daughter at my breast, reveling in the knowledge that I was feeding her from my own body. What a miraculous thing! I was mostly kidding about feeling like a Jersey cow. I loved being a mother, but couldn't deny I was exhausted. Olivia was a good baby, but even good babies need to eat every four hours. Jack came in and double-checked that I had some juice to sip while I nursed, then grabbed a pillow off the sofa, stretched out at my feet, and promptly fell asleep. I struggled to stay awake, at least until I moved Olivia to the other breast. I could hear the lawn mower outside. My son had gladly taken over the chore for his father, even after an exhausting soccer practice. Kai had grown and filled out a good deal over the past five years, and had made the varsity team as a sophomore at the high school he and Megan attended. In spite of her desire to sleep, I could hear Megan puttering in the kitchen, no doubt starting dinner, as she did frequently since Olivia's birth. I had learned to cook slightly better in the last few years, but I would never be cordon bleu quality, by any means.

As I looked at my husband, crashed on the floor, heard my son outside mowing the lawn, my sister-in-law prepping dinner in the kitchen, and my daughter falling asleep at my breast, I thought I must be the luckiest woman in the entire world. I had so much love in my life. I reached up to wipe away the tear—a happy one—that ran down my cheek. Life was so good.

THE END

Acknowledgments

Here we are at the end of the Seeker Series and I have to admit I'm kind of sad about it! Jack and Ally and all the rest have become real to me over the past year and a half and it's hard to let them go. But all good things must come to an end…until the spinoff series, that is!

There are so many people to thank for their help and support during this process! First, I'd like to thank the folks at NaNoWriMo (http://nanowrimo.org/) for what they do to encourage people to write their novels. On November 1, 2013, I had never seriously considered writing a novel. By November 30, 2013, I had the first 50,000 words of *Seeker* and a new passion for writing.

I also want to thank the team at Limitless Publishing. You gave me a chance and I can't begin to tell you all how much I appreciate it. From the amazing covers, careful editing, creative blurbs, and tireless marketing, this has been a wonderful experience and I look forward to more in the future.

My family has been super supportive in my writing endeavor and I love you all for it. My husband, Lyle, picks up the household slack and never complains that I write too much. My girls, Cat, Bri, and Lacey, are my beta-readers and sounding boards. Mom, Betty, Merle, Jeanette, Sheila: thanks for reading and telling me you enjoy my stories. Merle, I'm working on one without the paranormal, just for you.

So many of my friends have been wonderful throughout this process. Carol, I have no words. Just thank you. Mark, your encouragement means a lot. Michelle, you are my best cheerleader! Jen, thanks for being a fan! John and Shawna, you guys rock! Thanks to you all!

More than anything, I want to thank my readers. You guys are awesome and it's such a privilege to connect with you and hear what you think about my stories. Thanks!

About the Author

Amy Reece lives in New Mexico with her incredible husband and two ridiculous mutts, Greta and Sodapop. When she's not writing, she's teaching high school English and social studies or maybe wandering through a thrift store in search of the next lucky teapot for her vast collection. She is an unrepentant bookaholic and has overflowing bookshelves in nearly every room of her house. Her favorite authors include J.R.R. Tolkien, J.K. Rowling, and C.S. Lewis–must have something to do with initials! She loves to travel and is hoping to need many research trips for future writing projects.

Facebook:
https://www.facebook.com/areeceauthor

Twitter:
https://twitter.com/AReeceAuthor

Blog:
https://amyreece.wordpress.com/

Goodreads:
https://www.goodreads.com/author/show/13884337.Amy_Reece

Pinterest:
https://www.pinterest.com/alreece12/